There was nothing for it but for her to brazen it out.

"And where are you off to with your merry little band?" Max drawled.

Amity gritted her teeth at his bantering tone and raised her chin with great dignity. "I am for home," she said.

"Can I assume you are accompanied by a new addition to our happy household?"

"Yes, milord. I have just purchased the mare."

"Plans for a stud farm?" he asked.

"She needs a home," Amity said quietly.

"So it would seem." Max, his face a bland mask, stared at the horse, the abigail, and the mangy dog. "Mayhap in your busy schedule you might find time to have a brief chat with me in the library? I shall, of course, await your pleasure," Max said in a stream of ice. "Good day, Miss Fraser."

THE PERFECT FIANCÉE

Martha Jean Powers

FAWCETT CREST • NEW YORK

A Fawcett Crest Book
Published by Ballantine Books
Copyright © 1989 by Martha Jean Powers

Library of Congress Catalog Card Number: 88-92203

ISBN: 0-449-21639-X

Manufactured in the United States of America

First Edition: April 1989

To:
Lynn, David and the elusive Pablo
For:
Cedar Point and Clue, Circus Court and the Triumph
Closets and the full moon.

Chapter One

"You mean you've kept the girl a prisoner for eleven years?" Devereaux Havenhurst's raised voice indicated his astonishment as he stared across the room at his host. "Really, Max. Even for you that is a tawdry admission."

Lord Maxwell Kampford picked an invisible speck of lint from his black velvet sleeve. His dark head was bent as though he were totally engrossed in the task, but the tension in his body belied that charade. Max brushed the nap of the sleeve, then nodded as if satisfied and lifted his green eyes to his friend. "I have hardly held the girl prisoner, Dev. I am her guardian and I have done my best to keep Miss Fraser safe from the corrupting influences of society."

"Cut line, old son." Dev raised his snifter of brandy and waved it in Max's direction. "Perhaps you'd care to pull my other leg."

Max glowered at Devereaux. The man was sprawled in a high backed chair, one leg dangling over the arm and swinging back and forth as though wafted by some gentle breeze. The shock of white hair above dark eyebrows was always surprising in a man in his early thirties. At twenty Dev's hair had begun to show signs of premature aging much to the amusement of his friends, who referred to him thereafter as the Gray Fox.

Max had been pleased when Dev had arrived at Edgeworth and they had spent a long evening reminiscing about their salad days, but as his oldest friend, Dev was far too perceptive by half. Max's frown began to crumble and a sheepish expression crossed his face.

"Perhaps you're right. I was trying to put a good face on my behavior." Max pulled at his earlobe as he threw himself into the companion chair across from Dev.

"I had forgotten you even had a ward," Dev mentioned in some chagrin.

"To be perfectly blunt, so had I," Max muttered, his voice barely audible at such a bald admission.

Max shifted uncomfortably under the condemning glare of his friend. If he had been hoping for some sympathy he was well out. And in truth he could find little to excuse in his own behavior.

"Her parents died eleven years ago. I was nineteen and little used to children," Max said, only too aware of the defensive note that crept into his voice. "The Frasers had been friends of my parents for years. I myself had never met them. Both Frasers were killed in a carriage accident just after my own parents died. My father had been named as guardian to their daughter, and as his heir the guardianship had devolved to me. At the tender age of twenty-one I was appalled to discover I was responsible for the social, physical, and financial welfare of a ten-year-old girl."

"What was she like?"

"When I saw Miss Fraser at the time of her parents' funeral, she was a gawky thing. A thoroughly unprepossessing child."

"Most girls are at ten. No bosom and little bottom," Dev commented bluntly.

"The child was blessed with few charms and an impossible name. I cannot believe anyone would name a child Endurance. Endurance Fraser."

For the first time since Max began telling him about his ward, Dev's face lightened at the look of consternation on his friend's face. "Can I trust she was nothing like her name?"

"Little hope of that, old chap. Nervous sort of child, ever darting about like a hound who's lost the scent. Had a tendency to knock things over every time she moved. The day of the funeral she tripped on the hem of her dress and broke a vase when she waved her hand. Seemed all arms and legs, a white face, and an unruly wealth of bright red hair."

"Sounds perfectly charming, Max. No wonder you took her to your heart."

The biting sarcasm had little effect on Max, whose eyes were fixed on a spot above the Adam's fireplace. In his mind he could see the girl clearly, and when he spoke his voice was soft with remembrance.

"The child had enormous eyes which stared at me without blinking. They were the clearest blue. Dark, like a Scottish lake. Endurance stood in front of the desk as I told her what provisions had been made for her. No tears. No emotion. Just stared at me. Surely an unnatural attitude." Max stood up and reached for the snifter of brandy on the mantel. He took a sip, staring down reflectively into the amber liquor. "I told her I was sorry about her parents and she nodded but otherwise showed no change in expression. I asked her if she had any questions and she said no. She whirled around, knocked over a table, and left the room."

"Did she show to better advantage the next time?" Dev asked.

"That was the only time I have seen Endurance Fraser," Max answered stiffly.

"Devil you say!"

"What was I to do? I was twenty-one and a bachelor. Hardly the proper household to bring a child into. There was no other family to take her. I was already guardian to my eleven-year-old brother and he was off at school. I did what I could for the girl. I provided a safe, secure environment for her. Educated her. Even sent her presents at Christmas time."

"What on earth did you send the child, knowing her so little?"

"Books," Max mumbled, ignoring the snort of derision from his companion.

"Self-improvement books, I have little doubt." The words apparently hit the mark, for Max winced and Dev smiled grimly.

"Believe me, Dev, I thought I was doing my best for the girl. I will admit I was ill prepared to take on the responsibility of the child. At the time of the funeral, I set everything in train with my business manager, including the sending of Christmas presents." Then in a burst of honesty, "I thought to arrange the chit's life suitably so that I would not be bothered with further details. Since everything ran so smoothly the first year, I let my business manager deal with it. Eventually I forgot all about her."

Silence filled the room except for the soft crackle of the fire. It was not an easy silence; condemnation hung heavily between the two friends. Dev stared thoughtfully at Max whom he had known since they were boys in school together.

At thirty-two Max appeared cynical, arrogant, and uncaring. Beneath the elegant, black velvet jacket his body was surprisingly muscular. He had the tall, deceptively lean appearance of his father and he moved with the grace and balance of an athlete. His mother had bestowed the curly chestnut hair that was slicked smoothly away from his broad forehead. Dev missed the mischievous sparkle in Max's green eyes that used to lighten his somber childish face. The jaded stare through which he viewed the world now held little of the childish glint. Max had seen too much to find the world amusing. His eyes were shaded, giving little evidence of his true feelings, but Dev knew him well and sensed a vulnerability behind the icy gaze.

For a moment Dev wondered about the orphan, Endurance Fraser. He could not imagine how the child had turned out. She would be twenty-one now. A woman grown. For eleven years she had been kept in virtual seclusion on an isolated estate in the north of England with no one but the servants for companions. Annoyance at his friend's neglect forced him to speak in a chill voice. "And by what miracle have you been reminded of the existence of the girl?"

Max's eyes flicked to Dev's face, and he nodded once as though accepting the condemnation he saw there. "My business manager came to me yesterday and asked me what arrangements I had made for the girl's come-out."

"And?"

"Devil take it, Dev! No need to come that toffy-nosed tone with me. Your life has hardly been such a model of exemplary behavior."

Max leaned against the mantel, his back to his friend. In frustration he kicked out at the andirons. A shower of ashes covered the toes of his polished Hessians, and he bent to restore order with the aid of a snowy white handkerchief. He buffed the boot until it shone with a mirrored patina. It was this familiar reminder of Max's fastidiousness that broke the spell of tension for Dev.

"You have the right of it, old man," he said, getting to his feet and placing a comradely hand on his friend's shoulder. "We have both done some incredibly stupid things so it is of little advantage for either to act the judge. To make amends I promise to listen without comment."

"No need for such sacrifice," Max said, grinning in relief. "If I wanted a sycophant, I would call in my butler. No need to spare your sharp tongue. I have been berating myself all day and it will be a relief to hear another voice."

After pouring more brandy, they retired to their chairs in greater charity with each other. Max sipped the liquor, rolling it over his tongue and relishing the sharp bite. He was delighted that Dev

was here to listen to his plans. He had not orga-
nized much as yet, but his friend's quick eye for
detail should catch any glaring errors of omission
in his stratagem.

"What exactly are your plans for the girl?" Dev
asked.

"To be perfectly honest, I have only just begun to
formulate some sort of campaign. Endurance is
twenty-one. It seems to me the proper thing would
be to give the chit a season in London and hope that
I can locate some poor sod to marry her and take
over the responsibility for the girl. She has been
well educated and is well dowered so I should have
no trouble finding a suitable party. I have sent my
coach to retrieve her. . . ."

"Really, Max," Dev interrupted. "She's not a
hunting dog."

"You have not seen her to make that assump-
tion."

"Neither have you in eleven years," Dev drawled.
"Girls change remarkably in that span of years."

"If you are hoping for some pink and white sim-
pering chit to suddenly spring up before your eyes,
you are doomed to disappointment. The most I can
expect is that she will not set London ablaze by
knocking over every candelabra she comes in contact with before I can get her married."

Dev chuckled at the description. "If you are taking her up to London, you will have to arrange for
a chaperon."

"I have given that some thought," Max said,
grimacing to indicate his enthusiasm for the project. "My cousin lives nearby and when I ap-

proached her, she agreed to act in that capacity.
You remember Lady Hester Grassmere?"

"The Ghost of Grassmere?"

Max smiled at the childhood nickname for his
cousin Hester. Dev and he had dubbed her thus for
her ability to sit unnoticed in a room, swathed in
gray dresses of a sameness to make her almost invisible. She spoke only in a whisper and was largely
ignored by most of the family.

"Unless your ward is a tiger, your cousin Hester
will make the perfect chaperon. Lord knows she is
the soul of propriety. I must confess, Max, that I
am impressed with how quickly you have moved to
make amends for your, if you will pardon my plain
speaking, your neglect of Miss Fraser." Dev tipped
an imaginary hat to his friend. "There is of course
one problem. Who will sponsor the girl for the season?"

Max hesitated before he responded. A grin split
his face, erasing some of the arrogance from his
countenance. "I will."

Dev threw his head back, giving in to a great
shout of laughter. "By gad, sir. I almost expect to
hear the walls of the gambling hells tumbling down
with the conversion of one of their favorite rakes
to the ranks of the respectable. I truly wish I were
going to be in London to see you bear leading the
chit."

"You won't be in London?" Max asked in some
surprise. "I was rather counting on you to stand as
friend."

"I am always that," Dev responded warmly.
"However, I shall be moldering at the stud farm at
Dunton House."

"Not a repairing lease, I trust."

"No. All's well in that quarter. It is a much happier reason. To the everlasting despair of my cousin Ponsonby, my darling Jena is going to present me with an heir."

"What ho, Dev! That's splendid news indeed." Max raised his snifter in salutation. "And just how long were you going to wait to inform me of such felicitous news?"

"I was trying to find a peaceful moment in our long reminiscing."

"And Jena? Is she well?"

"Disgustingly healthy. And quite typically, the bold baggage has informed me that it is an entirely natural process and there is no need to cosset her. Frankly she's much more worried about the brood mares on her confounded stud farm. She is busy as ever with that pet project and refuses to consider curtailing any of her activities. The exasperating minx even resists my entreaty to give up riding. If things progress as usual, I suspect my son or daughter will be born on horseback."

Max chuckled at the doting tone of his friend's voice. A smile tugged at his mouth as he recalled the turbulent beginning of the Gray Fox's marriage. "How goes your grandfather?"

"The Duke of Wayfield is ever on our doorstep. The old curmudgeon loved Jena from the first moment he saw her. If you recall, it was he who set seal on the marriage, and now he is content to crow over how well everything has turned out."

"I see Dickon occasionally. His girth is monumental and his taste for the ladies has not abated. Seems to cater to both appetites with continued gusto. Reggie has been little in evidence. Do you have news of him?" Max asked.

"Ah, my dear," Dev sighed heavily but his blue eyes sparkled with amusement. "There is nothing more threatening to a man's bachelor friends than a happily married woman. My docile Jena," he held up a hand at Max's snort of derision, "has turned into an indefatigable matchmaker. She is capitalizing on Reggie's penchant for blondes. It is only a matter of time before the man joins the ranks of the eternally damned breed of hag-ridden husbands. Jena will accept nothing less."

Max noted the softness on Dev's face as he spoke of his wife of two years. He seemed revoltingly contented with his lot in life. In fact, it was this very contentment that had forced Max to wonder if one could marry and still maintain a modicum of happiness.

For years Max had fought the idea of marriage. At a very early age he had realized that all was not well with his parents' relationship. There were continual arguments between the two, and eventually it became apparent that the source of contention was his mother's lack of fidelity. When he was ten, Max had awakened from a severe nightmare and fled to his parents' bedroom for comfort, only to discover his mother in bed with one of the footmen. His brother Philip had been born that same year, and although Max loved the child dearly, he wondered exactly who had fathered the child. Apparently Max's father was never convinced of the boy's paternity because he totally ignored the existence of the lad.

Max grew to manhood and watched as his father

took to drink and his mother continued her affairs. She was always surrounded by a coterie of men, the flame to their mothlike eagerness. He had done what he could to protect his brother's illusions but his own were scattered in the dust. When Max was twenty-one, his father, tired of playing the cuckold, shot his mother and then turned the gun on himself. Although the story was put about that they had died of a putrid fever, there were many who knew or at least suspected the actual facts.

Responsibility was the key word of Max's existence. Lately he had given much thought to the responsibility that he owed to the line. He considered it time that he set up his nursery, but he was loath to take the first step on the road to parson's mousetrap. In some respects he felt that the reminder of the existence of his ward was the goad he needed to move forward in his own life.

"From your appearance this evening, Max, it would appear that you have given up setting the hearts of the macaroni set aflutter," Dev drawled, black eyebrow cocked in question. He had not seen much of Max in the past year and he could not fail to notice the change. A year earlier his friend had cultivated the appearance of a dandy, wearing outlandish clothes and giving the impression that he had more hair than wit. Now he was dressed with an understated elegance that almost verged on the austere. "Does this mean that we shall never see the Pomona green satin ensemble that so offended my eyes?"

"It was only the waistcoat you were so disdainful of," Max declared in defense.

"Ah, yes. It was monstrously wonderful. Peacocks on the strut, was it?"

"Or some such. Much to my dismay, the younger set began to copy my every outfit and they did not have the panache to carry off the conceit." Max drew himself up, staring down his finely sculpted nose at his grinning friend. "Now I have adopted a new style. Like the Beau, simplicity is my watchword."

"Better not let Jena catch sight of your new distinguished looks. She will be trotting out the local maidens for your approval, and before you know it you will be leg-shackled."

Max cleared his throat, hesitating only slightly before he spoke. "In actual fact, I have decided to seek a wife."

"I say, Max. Don't tell me you have fallen prey to a pair of *beaux yeux*?"

"I am far too cynical to be taken in by mere beauty," Max smiled. "I am considering marriage because I think it is the proper thing to do. For the line, don't you know. Besides, a wife would be extremely helpful in bringing out my ward."

Save for one arched eyebrow, Dev's face showed little change of expression. " 'Pon rep, old man, that does seem extreme measures just to fire off the chit."

"Give over, do. I have given this serious consideration, Dev." Max stood up and, with his hands behind his back, began to pace the floor much like a harried professor. "With brother Philip away with the army, I must make certain to secure the line."

"How is the young scamp?" Dev asked.

"Much as usual. He has discovered other officers

of similar vein, and they are bent on wreaking havoc on the female population of foreign lands. His letters mention little of battle, but the home office has kept me apprised of his actions. Been mentioned in dispatches several times," Max said with pardonable pride.

"I hear the corps de ballet wore black arm bands for a week when you bought him his colors."

"Shouldn't doubt it for a moment," Max said ruefully. He faced Devereaux, his face a picture of arrogant disdain. "Surely, Dev, we were not such ramshackle fellows."

When Max's face split into a wide grin and laughter filled the room, Dev was reminded of his friend in their more youthful days. Of late Max had become more sarcastic and arrogant; there was little of the carefree boy he had originally known. And now this latest start.

"Do not keep me on the edge of my chair, old man. What is all this about a bride?"

Max executed a military turn on the carpet and stood still, facing his friend. His face was grave, his mouth pulled into sober lines. "I lead a very well-ordered life, Dev. It is my heritage from a rather ragtag existence as a child. I have learned that logical planning is the key to success in any venture and I have applied it in every avenue of my life."

"Yes, I recall rejoicing in your methodical planning of our most devilish campaigns," Dev agreed dryly.

Max ignored the interruption, so involved was he in his own thoughts. "Marriage is strictly a business arrangment for the mutual benefit of both parties. The groom gains the possibility of an heir, while the bride, in most cases, receives financial security. Therefore, it is only a matter of keeping one's wits about one in making a choice." Max began to pace again, occasionally turning to Dev to punctuate a point with a deliberate jerk of his head. "I have considered the qualities I require in a wife, and all I need do is locate a young lady with the proper credentials and I will have discovered the perfect fiancée."

Dev shook his head in dismay. His friend seemed to think one should enter into marriage in a most logical way. Dev's marriage had been most illogical and he had never been happier. He too had been a cynic, but he knew very well the joy to be had in being in love with the woman one married. Max was due for great disappointment if he planned to conduct a courtship with methodical precision.

"Then while you are shepherding your ward to the social functions of the season, you will be on the lookout for a suitable wife?" Dev asked.

"Exactly," Max answered, grinning broadly in the face of his friend's apparent skepticism. "Truly, Dev, finding a wife is no different from purchasing a horse. There are bloodlines to consider, spirit, manners, and, of course, health. Lately I have given some thought to the sterling qualities of a young lady of my acquaintance. Naturally there is nothing settled as yet."

"Good Lord," Dev muttered. "And did you check her teeth?"

"I take my responsibilities to the family line quite seriously," Max said defensively. "I do not choose to make the same mistake my father did."

"At the rate you're going, Max, you will make a

far graver one," Dev snapped. "All right, I shall not twit you for such pomposity. Hopefully you will find happiness with this businesslike attitude. Who is this delightful paragon of virtue?"

"Honoria Waterston." Max rolled the name off his tongue as though testing the air with the sound. His eyes were distant as he tried to see into the future with the bride of his choice, so he missed the start of dismay on his friend's face at the mention of the name. "I have found her to be a proficient hostess, a properly mannered young lady, and a decidedly lovely one to boot."

"I would have to agree," Dev said aloud, although there was little agreement in his mind. Several years ago it had been apparent to everyone in society that Honoria had set her cap for Max and had been waging a nonstop campaign ever since. Dev had never liked the young woman, with her cold blue eyes and false modesty, and found it hard to believe that Max had not seen her for the manipulative schemer she was.

"This situation should not affect my commitment to Endurance," Max added hastily. "I have already enlisted Honoria's help in her behalf. I am sure Endurance will appreciate a knowledgeable woman her own age as a friend and confidante."

Dev had difficulty containing a snort of derision at the blindness of his friend. Honoria never permitted friendships with other women who might compete for a share of her spotlight. She had obviously agreed to play Lady Bountiful in order to further convince Max of her suitability as a wife.

"I think, Dev, that this season should run quite smoothly," Max stated. "Unless Endurance is a complete antidote, I should be able to look over her prospects and come up with an acceptable match for her. In the meantime I will have plenty of opportunity to consider Honoria's suitability as my wife."

"Have you given no consideration to the possibility that you might look for a woman to love?"

"Love is not a proper requisite for entering into a lifelong contract," Max answered pompously.

"Two years ago I might have agreed with your assessment, but now that I have experienced the absolute bliss of a loving relationship, I find I cannot concur." Dev's face was troubled as he looked with fondness at his old friend. "As you know, I scoffed at love, but I can honestly say that without Jena I would find little to convince me of the value of life. She is a constant joy to me, Max."

"I admit you have found happiness with Jena, but she is truly unique. I have vast experience with women and feel I understand them quite well." Hearing a loud moan, Max stared at his friend in surprise.

"Now I know you have lost what little sense you possess," Dev stated, rolling his eyes to the ceiling. "Any man who announces he understands women is surely doomed. The good Lord never intended us to understand, merely to enjoy."

Max waved his hand as if dismissing all his friend's arguments. "It is my way, old thing. I have arranged my life to function like a well-oiled machine. I do not want the disruptions and turmoils so common to the state of lovesick swains. Each of my estates is run precisely to my specifications. My town house is Spartan, orderly, and easy to maintain. I want no confusion in my life."

"Sometimes there is great happiness in confusion."

"Perhaps for some," Max conceded. "But for me, I go the reasonable route. One need only realize that making a proper marriage is not unlike an important purchase. One must select the merchandise with great care to avoid flaws in the materials. Careful consideration is always the best plan."

Having been married for two years, Dev was wise enough to realize that where men and women were concerned things seldom ran according to plan. A low-cut dress and a pair of mischievous eyes could generally work havoc on the best of intentions. Dev's face registered concern that his friend should so blithely discount the joys of love. He could only hope that the season ahead would produce some young deb who, for Max, might turn out to be the perfect fiancée.

Chapter Two

"Remind me to keep my hands quiet and a still tongue in my head," Amity cried, wriggling restlessly on the carriage seat. "It's all so exciting, but I must admit I am a trifle nervous. How will I remember all the lessons on proper etiquette, Muffin?"

Receiving only a snore in reply, Endurance Amity Fraser turned to stare out the carriage window. Not that she ever thought of herself as Endurance. She much preferred her second name and had adopted it for her own. Sometimes it was difficult to respond, since no one at Beech House ever called her anything but Endurance. Amity thought the name sounded like some squinty-eyed spinster who would wear drab bombazine and a look of martyrdom etched on her face.

She grinned impishly as the carriage hit a particularly nasty pothole, jolting her companion on the seat. The additional movement had little effect on the sleeper, and with a sniff of annoyance, Amity let her thoughts wander to her coming meeting with her guardian. Perhaps in eleven years she had changed enough to find favor in his eyes. She was only too aware that she could never claim to be a beauty. Red hair, freckles, and pale white skin on a tall frame were definitely not in vogue, Amity thought, wrinkling her tip-tilted nose in dismay. She could only hope that she would make a better impression on him than she had the first time.

Amity could remember her one and only interview with her guardian. The evening of her parents' funeral, after all the mourners had left, she had been called to the library to meet with Lord Max. Although she had seen him during the day, there had been so many people milling around the manor house that she had not spoken to him except to receive his condolences.

Closing her eyes, Amity could bring back the scene in the library with total clarity. Max had been sitting at her father's desk, dressed in his funeral black, face composed into the expected sober lines. He had looked up apprehensively when she entered the room, as though he expected her to break into tears or fall down in a fit. Amity recalled forcing herself to remain expressionless, although inside she was quaking with fear and loneliness. She would have liked nothing better than to curl up on his lap, place her head on his chest, and feel the warmth of his arms around her. Perhaps if he had been older, but Max was a young man forced to take on the responsibility of a ten-year-old girl. He would be embarrassed at such a display of emotion. So Amity had composed her expression and waited with anticipation for him to explain his plans for her.

As Max surveyed her from her flyaway red curls

to her scuffed half boots, Amity could see equal
parts of disappointment and distaste mirrored in
the green depths of his eyes. She had straightened
her spine and shrugged away the suspicion of tears
that threatened to rain down her cheeks. By her
bravery alone she hoped to prove her worthiness.
But all her stratagems were to no avail. She would
have no new home. Max was leaving her at Beech
House, where she had been born and had lived for
ten years.

After Max became her guardian, and despite her
original disappointment, Amity began to hope that
her life would change for the better. For two years
she had looked forward to Christmas, when she assumed that he would invite her to his home residence so she might partake of the festivities among
family and friends. There had been no invitation,
just a gaily wrapped box of books. As the third
Christmas arrived, she had buried her hopes, determined to create her own memories instead of de-
pending on others. From then on she was able to
open, without anger or frustration, the box of books
Max sent as a suitable present. She found amusement in his choice of self-improvement books and
chuckled at their reading.

Aside from the Christmas books, never once in
the last eleven years had she received a letter, a
gift, or a visit from her guardian. All instructions
as to her care and education were sent directly to
Mrs. Dimwittier, the housekeeper, and thus to the
current governess, who passed on what information
she thought proper to Amity. At first Amity had
been hurt, but, never prone to self-pity, she eventually realized that a young man would have little

in common with a child. Yet it would have been nice if he had taken just a little bit of an interest in her.

"What a time to sleep, Muffin. I really could use someone to talk to," Amity muttered in exasperation.

The recipient of these words lifted sleepy lids for a brief moment, then sighed heavily and drifted off again. The young girl made a moue of annoyance and returned to her examination of the rolling countryside.

Once Amity realized there was no one who really cared for her, she had taken control of her life. She no longer expected love, so she was free to make friends without fear of rejection. She was surrounded by servants, and she talked with them, unfettered by the conventions and taboos of society. She made friends in the village and over the years met nothing but kindness. Innately curious and impetuous, her days were happily occupied with studies, reading, and friends on the estate or in the village.

Only in her dreams did she yearn for a different life. She desired a real home with a husband and a child of her own. And she dreamed of Max. She did not blame him for leaving her at Beech House. She understood that he was too busy to be bothered about her, but she wished it had been otherwise. For years Amity dreamed that he would return and rescue her from her bleak existence. A knight on a ferocious white charger saving the damsel in distress.

Amity snorted at her ridiculous fancies, and felt a return of the nervous flutter in the region of her stomach at the thought of her journey's end. She listened intently to the rhythm of the carriage horses, fearful that one of the beasts might be going lame, but the noble cattle drew her steadily toward her new home and a guardian she had only seen once.

"Come on, Muffin, you lazy slug. Wake up," Amity muttered, elbowing her companion mercilessly. When this tactic had little effect, she leaned over and whispered coaxingly, "I'll help you look for cats. And maybe even a rabbit."

Thus tempted, Amity's companion, an enormous brown dog of unknown, and highly suspect, origin, yawned hugely, his great tongue arching upward between neat rows of white teeth. He stretched all four legs and emitted a low rumbling moan before he turned his head toward his mistress. Slowly Muffin's eyelids raised, and he stared at Amity through soulful pools of brown.

"What a lump you are," Amity said as she hugged her friend, nuzzling one floppy ear. "Ever since we got in the coach this morning, you've been sleeping. Besides we're almost there. Coachman said it would only be another half hour."

Thus reminded of their imminent arrival, Amity bit her lip, feeling the jolt of her accelerated heartbeat. She pushed the huge dog off her lap and brushed frenziedly at the clumps of dog hair left behind. Then reaching up, she untied the blue ribbon that confined her hair at the nape of her neck. As usual a cloud of the bright red curls had escaped and were billowing around her cheeks. Quickly she raked her fingers through the shimmering mass of waist-length hair and retied the ribbon more snugly.

"My reticule! My gloves!" she wailed, looking frantically around the carriage.

She found the reticule at last beneath the plain poke bonnet, which she jammed casually on her head, but after a hurried search could not find her mittens. She vaguely remembered removing them at the last stop, and accepted the sad fact that she would have to arrive at her destination with bare hands. The reticule was dusty, and she grasped the strings and smacked it briskly against the squabs, sending up clouds of dust. Muffin inhaled and sneezed so heartily that the movement propelled the dog upright, where he sat, eyes wide open and black nose aquiver. When Amity giggled at the dog's expression, he looked so offended that she burst into a loud whoop of laughter. Thus Amity and Muffin arrived at Edgeworth.

When the liveried footman pulled down the stairs and opened the door, he was confronted by the laughing countenance of a redheaded girl and a low growl from her companion. Hastily he backed away, bowing as he said, "Welcome to Edgeworth, Miss Fraser."

From a safe distance the footman surveyed the young lady. Told to expect Lord Kampford's ward, he had been picturing a small child, not this lovely young woman. There was still a hint of gangly awkwardness in her movements, but like a young colt, thoroughbred lines were apparent. Her body was tall and slightly but softly rounded; her hands and feet were small and elegant. She wore a carriage dress and matching cape in a muted blue color that was well made and sensible rather than the height of fashion.

The young footman extended his hand, but the young lady bounded out of the coach without assistance. Her lightly freckled face was still flushed with laughter, and her white teeth flashed in an open smile that quite won the heart of the boy.

"Thank you for the greeting. I'm so glad to be here at last," Amity said, her voice still bubbling with amusement. Then with a swirl of cape, she turned back to the coach to fetch her friend. "Out, Muffin."

The dog remained upright on the seat, looking in no hurry to leave the comfortable confines of the carriage for unknown, and possibly unwelcome, surroundings.

"Come on, you great looby," Amity hissed, glancing in embarrassment at the footman. In explanation, she said, "Muffin is rather shy, uh . . ."

"Peter, Miss," the boy answered, bobbing his head in greeting. "It takes some that way. Would you like me to fetch him?"

Since Muffin had begun to growl again, there was a slight hesitancy in the footman's voice. Quickly Amity said, "Thank you, Peter, but he's more used to me."

Amity scrambled inelegantly up the stairs and grasped a handful of fur at Muffin's neck. With her hip she shoved the dog off the seat and half dragged, half carried the reluctant visitor to the carriage sweep. Peter shifted nervously, but, pluck to the bone, he extended his open palm for the inspection of the huge dog. Muffin sniffed cautiously, then extended his tongue and licked the footman's hand.

"Muffin obviously approves, Peter. And he's very particular about his friends." Amity smiled at the relieved look on the footman's face, but in an instant it had changed to red-faced embarrassment. Turning, she was unabashed to discover the dog had given in to an urgent call of nature. Lowering her voice, she said to the footman, "Truly, Muffin usually behaves with more discretion, although I suspect my guardian will not be best pleased to have the wheels of his carriage abused in such a fashion."

Peter smothered a laugh, amazed at the matter-of-fact way the young lady spoke of the subject. There seemed to be nothing hoity-toity about his lordship's ward, and he resolved to help her when he could.

Amity called to the dog, then her eyes shifted to the imposing facade of the great house and she shivered, slightly intimidated by the grandeur of the estate. Hesitantly she said, "Well, I suppose I better go in."

Reminded of his duties, Peter stiffened to attention, extending his hand in the direction of the opened double doors. Under his breath he blurted, "Putnam will have my head, miss, for keeping you jawing on the very steps."

"I suppose that's the very proper butler I see waiting inside," Amity whispered.

"Aye, Miss Fraser. Him and the housekeeper, Mrs. Trilby, will be greeting you proper-like."

"Sounds awful," Amity moaned, earning a wink of encouragement from the boy before he turned back to the coach and the other footmen, who were struggling to remove her trunks from the boot.

Shifting her reticule to her left hand, she grasped

a great chunk of Muffin's hair and hauled the dog up the shallow stone steps to the huge carved doorway. Her blue eyes widened at the line of servants spread across the marble foyer, and she hastily released the dog, wiping her hand surreptitiously on her skirt. A flush rose to her cheeks, but she gamely stepped forward to address the impressive figure at the head of the line.

Before she could speak, the butler clicked his heels lightly and inclined his upper body in greeting. "Welcome to Edgeworth, Miss Fraser."

"Thank you, Putnam. I'm very pleased to be here," Amity said, extending her hand to the startled butler, who shook it gingerly as though handling stolen goods.

"This is the housekeeper, Mrs. Trilby." Putnam indicated a plump, motherly woman whose work-roughened hands nervously gripped her ring of keys.

"I'm very glad to meet you, Mrs. Trilby." Amity grinned warmly at the woman, who responded with a tentative smile of her own.

"If you'd be kind enough to follow me, Miss Fraser," the housekeeper said.

Amity hesitated, knowing that the household's first impression of her was very important. As always, she responded to instinct and placed a detaining hand on the older woman's arm. "If it's all right, Mrs. Trilby, I'd like to meet the others first so that I can begin sorting out names."

The housekeeper's mouth opened, but no words came forth, and in desperation the woman turned for instruction. Putnam, more used to the idiosyncrasies of the gentry, coughed lightly. The line of servants snapped to attention. Punctiliously the starchy butler introduced each of the members of the downstairs brigade, while Amity smiled and shook hands, wondering all the while how she would ever remember all of their names. They had just reached Jem, the pot scrubber, when the boy's shoulders began to shake with barely controlled laughter.

Amity had been aware of Muffin's cringing presence as she walked down the line. However, she had tried to ignore him in order to maintain her dignity. Now at the touch of a cold nose on her leg, she realized the dog had gone to extreme measures to gain reassurance. Turning slightly, she looked down at the shaggy beast, whose head was hidden bashfully beneath her skirts. She could feel the hot color washing across her face, and she grasped Muffin's fur and tugged as her booted foot nudged his nose. Great, soulful brown eyes peered up at her, and she immediately dropped to her knees to hug the dog.

"I'm afraid Muffin is as nervous as I am, coming to our new home," Amity apologized to the ring of interested faces.

There was a murmur of low-voiced encouragement before Putnam extended his hand to help Amity to her feet. She murmured her gratitude as she, and the softly padding Muffin, followed Mrs. Trilby to the stone steps that swept up one side of the main hall. In her overly tired state she could not begin to focus on the myriad portraits that lined the stairs and the hallways they traversed. When the housekeeper finally stopped in front of a carved oak doorway, Amity sighed with relief.

"Lord Kampford said you were to have this room, miss."

As the door swung open, Amity emitted another

sigh, this time of deep contentment, and stepped cautiously on the exquisite oriental carpet. The room was square except for one corner, where a rounded wall of windows jutted out from the building. On the one side she could look out at the rambling rooftops that towered above her, and on the other side, the gardens were spread out for her view. The four-poster bed was hung with a billow of white material stitched with tiny violets. The windows were swathed in the same fabric, and the walls were covered with a pale lilac silk. Impulsively she turned to the housekeeper.

"I've never seen such a lovely room, Mrs. Trilby. I know I shall be very happy here."

The housekeeper's face softened at the glowing look of the young girl. She was like a breath of spring blowing through the old hall. It reminded her of how it used to be when Lord Max's mother was alive. For ten years there had been no laughter within the cold stone walls of Edgeworth. A shadow crossed the older woman's face, and she cleared her throat before she was able to speak.

"Will your abigail be following you, miss?" Mrs. Trilby asked.

"No, she, uh . . ." Amity hesitated, unwilling to lie. "I didn't have an abigail to bring. You see, I've never had one."

"Never, miss?" The housekeeper looked astounded at this information, but quickly recovered and ventured a suggestion. "Never mind, Miss Fraser. I'll take care of everything. While you're here, Pauline's the girl for you. Good-hearted as a nanny for all that she's only twenty. Has a brain in her head and a magical way with hair."

"She sounds wonderful," Amity said in relief.

"Naturally, I'll have to ask his lordship's permission," the housekeeper reminded the young girl, "but I'm sure he'll agree to the arrangement. For now, miss, why don't you lie down, and I'll send Pauline up in time to get you ready for dinner."

"Thank you, Mrs. Trilby, for all your kindness," she said to the startled woman who blushed, bobbed a curtsy, and exited hastily.

As she closed the door after the housekeeper, Amity looked around the room for Muffin. The lumbering beast had taken possession of the chaise longue along the wall. The curly brown fur looked ludicrous against the lilac and silver satin, but Muffin appeared totally contented with his long pointed muzzle resting comfortably atop a fringed throw pillow. Wearily Amity kicked off her half boots on her way to the bed and sank gratefully onto the counterpane, unable to exert the energy necessary to undress. Snuggling into the pillows, she closed her eyes, delighted that the bed did not buck and heave like the motion of the carriage.

Sleep evaded her as her mind began to wonder what the evening ahead would bring. She had been surprised that Lord Max had not met her himself. As her guardian, Amity thought he might have extended the courtesy. But then she knew so little of the ways of the upper classes, despite the fact she had been born into their ranks. In fact she knew practically nothing about her guardian. From things her governesses had said, Amity had learned that Lord Maxwell Kampford was heir to a vast fortune. He owned a house in London and several large estates, but Edgeworth was his preferred residence. From things left unsaid, she gathered that he was considered a prime catch on the marriage market, but preferred his relationships among the muslin trade. For the rest she would have to wait and see what his sudden interest in her meant.

Lord Kampford's letter had arrived out of the blue, and Amity was thrilled to discover her presence was requested at Edgeworth. Although the missive contained no specific information, there was much speculation at Beech House. While the servants and her latest governess/companion, Miss Endicott, packed her clothing, Amity met with the estate manager to prepare him for her absence. She had great faith in Henderson and knew he would care for the estate much as he always had. While Amity finished her packing, Miss Endicott fed her a continuous stream of strictures and aphorisms in a vain attempt to make up for any lapses in her pupil's education.

Amity was consumed by curiosity over Lord Maxwell's summons. She had assumed he had forgotten her existence and wondered what this reminder of his authority portended. She suspected he had decided she was of marriageable age and wished to discuss his plans for her. Although she might desire him to take a personal interest in her, her practical nature convinced her that Lord Max merely wanted to marry her off. She expected nothing else.

Amity knew from her childhood that it was useless to expect much. When she was quite young, she had expected that her parents would love her. It was finally borne in on her that her mother, dubbed "Goddess Divine" by the London dandies, was ashamed of her unbeautiful child. Her father was not fond of children. And, of course, she was only a girl. He saw her primarily as a means to make a favorable alliance, thus adding to his own consequence.

Her parents' disinterest in her, combined with Max's neglect after their deaths, forced her to depend on herself for enjoyment. Another child might have viewed the world with a jaundiced eye, but Amity found much pleasure in her solitary life. She had a keen sense of humor and a deep well of curiosity which helped her to find joy in the smallest incidents of her life. She had discovered early that she was responsible for her own happiness and as a consequence had grown into a cheerful and trusting person.

Amity flopped over on her back, staring up sightlessly at the fluffy canopy. She was sure she was too excited to sleep. She thought about all the new experiences that awaited her, and she wanted to shout in anticipation. The library at Beech House had been filled with books about London. Her curiosity had been whetted in the long, bleak winter evenings as she read of the wonders of the city. Although she had been happy enough at her parents' home, she had been starved of people to exchange ideas with and places to feed her desire for knowledge. There was a whole world waiting for her, and she was anxious to grasp it.

Muffin moaned and snuffled, no doubt dreaming of rabbits he could chase. Amity sighed softly as her mind drifted finally into sleep.

Chapter Three

"Well, miss, if you ask me, this is the only one what's fit to wear," Pauline said. It was apparent that Amity's new abigail was not overly impressed by the items in her wardrobe. With pursed mouth and narrowed eyes, she had examined each dress, finally deciding that the only possibility for the evening was a blue and green plaid wool with a high waist and a touch of white lace at the neck.

"Would you suggest I burn the rest?" Amity asked.

"Gor, miss!" Pauline whirled around, shocked by the thought of such dreadful waste. Her brown eyes took in the wide grin on her mistress's face, and she blinked. Catching the joke, she snorted aloud, hiding her laughter behind her hands. "Not that they don't deserve a proper funeral," she said when she could catch her breath.

"I know most of them are awful, Pauline, but there was not much need for fashion in the north. Warmth was much more important."

"Makes good sense, miss," Pauline agreed as she closed the doors of the wardrobe. "Soon you'll have new things, much more fitting for London. Mrs. Trilby said if I suit, I'll be your abigail while you're at Edgeworth."

"I'm sure we'll do fine together," Amity said. She had been pleased by the arrival of the cheerful, efficient girl. She was bony and plain of face, but her eyes, for all the sharpness of her glance, had the softness of a doe. Though younger by a year, Pauline had a worldly quality about her that convinced Amity she would be wise to heed the girl's suggestions.

She put herself in the servant's capable hands, and soon the room looked inhabited as she dressed for dinner. The only disagreement they had was at the abigail's suggestion of a more elaborate hairstyle than she was used to.

"I'm sure it would be lovely, Pauline, but I'd rather not put it up. My hair's so long that by the end of the evening, I'll have a pounding headache." Amity sat at the mirrored vanity and caught the disapproving expression of her new abigail. Coaxingly she added, "I promise you can concoct some fanciful creation at another time."

The girl's frown disappeared, and she brushed the long swath of hair until the red curls shone in the candlelight. "I have ever so many ideas, miss," Pauline said. "You have beautiful hair, but it could use a mite of trimming."

"This time I know you're right," Amity said laughing ruefully. "I've not been in society and so there's never been a need. This is just an informal dinner, so I'm sure no one will mind if my hair is undressed."

"The sash looks right perky." Pauline's voice

sounded as though she felt her new mistress needed encouragement.

After a cursory glance in the mirror, Amity stood up and shook out her skirt, searching the material for stray dog hairs. She had always liked the plaid dress; it was warm and comfortable. It had been perfect at Beech House with its long chilly corridors and drafty rooms. Granted, it was several years out of date, but then she had never cared that much about the current fashions. For the moment it would have to suffice. She knew her hair was neatly brushed, and her face was cleanly scrubbed. She suspected that due to her nervous state, her skin was paler tonight so that the freckles would stand out even more than normal. Shrugging, she turned to the dog sprawled in front of the door.

"Come on, Muffin," Amity said. The dog creakily pushed himself upright, his tail wagging in triumph at his accomplishment. He pressed his head against her knee, and Amity reached down to rub his neck. "Well, old friend, we don't want to make a bad impression by being late."

Thanking Pauline for all her help, Amity opened the door and started out into the hall. Although Muffin swung his head to follow her movements, the rest of his body remained firmly rooted to the floor. Returning, Amity grasped a handful of hair at his neck and kneed him gently toward the hall. Soulful brown eyes lifted to her face, and then, accepting the inevitable, the dog padded softly beside her toward the stairs. Luckily Peter, the helpful footman, was on duty in the foyer, and he indicated the double doors to the yellow salon. Two other footmen threw open the doors, and Amity braced herself, holding more tightly to Muffin.

When the doors opened, Max thought for a moment that he had been transported back in time. Framed by the heavily carved lintel, Amity looked like an ancient warrior queen, her hand resting on some noble beast. Crystal blue eyes, flashing with courage and intelligence, shone out of her white face. Burnished curls crowned her proudly raised head and fell in a cascade down her back. Max blinked and the magical vision was gone.

The girl hesitated in the doorway, her sparkling eyes flashing around the room in curiosity. Max was amazed that this was the same girl he had seen eleven years ago. His ward was not the pink and white debutante so much in fashion; she was a far more exotic creature. Her skin was too pale, her hair too red. Her mouth was too generous and her eyes too large. Each feature was discordant, but together they blended in a harmony of perfection. He wondered what had happened to the scrawny, clumsy child.

Max coughed sharply to remind the girl of her duty. She lowered her eyes modestly and came to stand in front of him. He was surprised at her height; somehow he had expected she would be tiny. The top of her head came above his shoulder, and he was six foot tall. He coughed once more, and she extended her hand, dropping into a curtsy. As Max bowed over her hand, she bobbed back up, her head crashing into his chin with a jolt that rattled every tooth in his head.

"Blast!" Amity said, blinking rapidly through the tears of pain as she held the sides of her head. Looking up through her blurred vision, she saw the pained look on the face of her guardian. And she had so wanted to make a good impression. Suddenly she was overcome by the humor of the situation.

As the pain of the blow began to wear off, Max glared at the clumsy girl. She had changed little since last he saw her. Visions of endless broken vases and knocked-over tables flashed before his eyes. Her come-out would be a debacle. He was much too old for such humiliation. He glowered down at the girl and watched the expressions flit across the too-open countenance: horror, embarrassment and then, of all things, amusement. When she started to laugh, he was surprised at the soft, lilting quality of her laughter.

"Only a harum-scarum girl would find amusement in such a social disaster." Max tried to keep his lips from twitching, but could not control the twinkle in his eyes.

"I really am most sorry, your lordship." Despite the sincerity of her words, Max noted the laughter in the crystal blue eyes. "Perhaps we might start over. Although I fear I must warn you I am not very expert." To her credit, she controlled her expression and dipped into a slightly more graceful curtsy, peeking up at him through a fringe of lashes.

In the grown woman Max well remembered the steady blue eyes of the child. Now there was a sheen of laugh-tears that gave them an uncanny brilliance, and he found himself disappointed when she lowered her lids, hiding them from him. He shook his head, narrowing his eyes at the taking child.

"Welcome to Edgeworth, Endurance."

"Thank you, my lord," Amity said demurely. She

liked his deep voice, which was rich and melodious for all that his words were stilted. She willed herself to say something else, but no words appeared in her mind, so for once she remained silent. A snore interrupted her, and she fought down another bout of giggles as she looked down at Muffin.

When Amity dipped into her curtsy, the traitorous dog took it as a sign that he could relax. He had flopped down directly in front of Max, who was now trapped against the fireplace. Amity nudged the dog with the toe of her slipper, knowing from experience that it was a useless gesture, but hopeful nonetheless. As expected, Muffin merely snuffled in his sleep.

"I'm sorry about Muffin, my lord. He's getting old and the journey tired him out. He's not much used to travel," Amity defended.

"Where did you get such a mangy beast?" Max asked, curious despite himself.

"He was abandoned on the roadside and near to death. He needed a home," she finished as if it were the most natural of occurrences.

"It is of no consequence," Max said dismissively. With caution he stepped over the recumbent figure and firmly grasped Amity's elbow. He turned her toward the other occupant in the room, and his ward quickly made another shaky curtsy. "Cousin Hester, this irrepressible child is my ward, Endurance Fraser. Lady Grassmere will be your chaperon during your stay here and during your come-out. Hopefully the three of us will survive the enterprise," he amended dryly.

Gray dress, gray face and gray hair. So self-effacing was Lady Grassmere that Amity thought it would be difficult to remember she was there. Looking more closely, she noted the gentle kindness in the woman's brown eyes and resolved to treat the older woman with great respect. She suspected Lady Grassmere would find the experience of chaperoning her a rather wearing affair.

"And I also bid you welcome to Edgeworth, my dear," Hester said. Her soft voice was just above a whisper and had the insubstantial quality of a summer breeze. "I met your mother many years ago. A lovely woman. I must admit, Endurance, that you are nothing like I had pictured."

"I'm sorry, milady." Amity hung her head in embarrassment. "I am so used to my looks that I forget what a disappointment I am to those who knew my mother."

"Disappointment, child?" Hester stared at the burnished head, wondering if she had heard correctly.

"I am nothing like my mother," Amity admitted.

"No, my dear, you are not," the old woman agreed. She had thought the girl's mother lovely, but shallow in the extreme. By the look of intelligent curiosity she had seen in the girl's eyes, Hester suspected the child had far greater depth. "You are, I would guess, quite unique."

Max was much struck by the interchange and it took him several minutes to take in the import of his ward's remarks. He opened his mouth to comment, but before he could speak, dinner was announced. Giving an arm to each of the ladies, he led them into the dining room.

The dinner progressed well, and Max led the conversation to discover the extent of Amity's educa-

tion and deportment. It appeared as though the
governesses he had provided had done well by the
girl. She was well-read, her conversation clearly
showing she was a gently reared young lady. He
noted she entered the discussions freely with perhaps a dash too much enthusiasm, but for the most
part, Max was pleased with the girl's manners and
ease of speech.

Continually through the meal Max's eyes were
drawn to the shining face of his ward. He was surprised at his own feeling of well-being, since he had
originally resented the appearance of the girl in his
bachelor life. There was definitely something vastly
appealing about the girl as he watched her fiery
curls nod at a question from Lady Grassmere. He
had been worried about sponsoring the girl, but
considered now that it might not be such a regret-
table experience. After her initial painful curtsy,
he recalled as he rubbed his chin, she had at least
not knocked anything over. If she could remain
seated through her come-out, he might fire her off
with little damage to vases, porcelain figurines and
other assorted bric-a-brac.

The dinner was a novelty to Amity, used to the
plain, nourishing fare that had been served up at
Beech House. At each remove she questioned the
footman about each dish, tasting a little of everything until she thought she might burst. She answered Max's questions and entered into the
conversation on books and history. It was at the
end of the meal that the subject turned to a discussion between Lady Grassmere and her guardian
over the latest opera fare. Amity was pleased to be

excluded since it gave her the opportunity to study Lord Max more closely.

She was pleased that her memory of him as a young man had not been faulty. He had been handsome then with his fine features and curly brown hair, but now his face had more character, a pride in himself that had been absent in his youth. He was tall and lean without appearing effete. He wore the black satin jacket and pantaloons with an air of elegance that owed nothing to his tailor. His waistcoat and linen were blindingly white. All his raiment was deceptively simple and without doubt incredibly expensive.

His eyes don't match, Amity thought to herself. Everything about him was extremely proper, almost arrogant. His words were sarcastic and at times carried a cutting sneer. It was only in his green eyes that Amity found a wariness, a hesitancy that surprised her. Although earlier she suspected that he might have found her amusing, there had also been puzzlement. It was almost as if he were unused to laughter.

After dinner Lady Grassmere sank into a chair beside the fireplace and took out her needlework. While she stitched, Max explained some of the plans that he had developed to launch her in society. She would remain at Edgeworth for several weeks while Lady Grassmere smoothed out some of her deficiencies in the art of social graces. Then they would remove to Max's town house in London for the season. Amity listened eagerly, interjecting an occasional excited question. She was especially pleased when he mentioned that his particular friend, Honoria, would stand as her friend.

"I will try very hard not to give her a disgust of me, milord," Amity said, her blue eyes serious for once.

"Just act natural, Endurance, and I am sure in a few days you will be bosom bows," Max answered confidently. "Have you any questions?"

"At the moment, your lordship, my head is whirling with excitement," Amity admitted. "Although there is something that I would like to ask. Would you find it terribly pushing of me if I changed my name?" At the surprised look on her guardian's face, she hurried into speech. "My second name is Amity and I much prefer it. Would it be quite honest if I used that name, your lordship?"

"Lord love you, child," Max said, chuckling at the request. "It shows you have much sense. Endurance, indeed. I will take great pleasure in erasing the name from my memory. And in turn you shall call me Max. Every time you say your lordship, I feel weighted down by another twenty years."

Amity smiled at her guardian, liking him very much better than she had expected. A snore from the direction of the fireplace alerted her to the fact that her chaperon had nodded off over her stitchery. Her eyes twinkled up at Max, and he responded in kind.

"Perhaps you would care to walk in the long gallery?" Max asked, extending his hand. "I find myself restless after dinner and have a need to stretch my legs."

She eagerly accepted his invitation, and soon they were strolling in front of a row of imposing portraits while Max entertained her with a history of his family. Amity could see that her guardian had inherited much of his good looks, and was especially pleased that so many of his ancestors had his unusual green eyes. She stood before the portrait done just after Max had inherited, and smiled at the slim, arrogant figure.

"Even then you were quite fierce, Max," Amity said.

"Fierce? Never say," Max drawled, enjoying the girl's concentrated gaze on his portrait. "I like to think I was feeling extremely elegant."

"That, too, of course, but there is the look of a rat terrier."

Max's chin raised in hauteur, and he was just about to bite out a choice set-down to the bold chit when he caught the gleam of laughter in her eyes. His own softened and he reached out to tweak her chin. "What a wretched child you are. With such an acid tongue, how am I ever to find a man to bring up to scratch?"

In the silence that followed, Amity's forehead puckered in concern. Taking her courage in hand, she asked the question that had been worrying her since she left Beech House. "Do you think someone might offer for me?"

"No need to fear, child," Max said, oddly touched by the look of strain on the girl's face. "I will not marry you off to the first eligible party. You will have plenty of time to enjoy the season."

"You mistake me, sir," Amity said. "I am eager to accept any proposal."

"You wish to marry?" Max could not really understand why anyone should wish to enter that unenviable state. "Why?"

"I would like to have a baby," Amity answered

without hesitation. When she noticed the rise of color in her guardian's face, she chuckled and reached out to pat the sleeve of his jacket. "I apologize for my plain speaking, sir, but you did ask."

"More fool I," he muttered under his breath. Drawing himself up, he tried to speak as casually as he could. "It is true that when you marry, a child follows shortly thereafter. No need to discuss any inconsistencies in that rule. Just take my word for it." It would seem that having a ward was not always clear sailing. He removed a spotless handkerchief and mopped his forehead before he could continue. As he returned the handkerchief to his pocket, he noted the amusement on the face of his ward. "Please tell me that you need no further information along these lines," he requested hopefully.

At his harried attitude Amity could not hold back her laughter. His expression changed to one of injury, and she tried to sober her own expression to salve his feeling of ill-usage. "Truly, Max, I promise I will ask you no more inconvenient questions. It must be a great trial for you to have a ward."

"I am just beginning to suspect as much," he answered, waggling his eyebrows until she burst into a stream of musical laughter. As he looked down at the girl, he realized that since Amity's arrival, he had only given cursory thought to the disadvantages of sponsoring the girl. For the most part he was enjoying himself, watching the fascinating creature who was Miss Amity Fraser.

"Perhaps we might return to the salon to continue this discussion. I have the feeling I might require something strengthening to drink." Max pulled Amity's hand through his arm and turned

her back along the hallway. "The noble Putnam
will bring the tea tray and some brandy, and you
shall tell me why you are in such a hurry to marry
and set up a nursery."

Lady Grassmere woke when the butler brought in
the tray, and Amity served the old woman, taking
time to praise the chair cover she was working on.
The stitchery was precise, but the picture was an un-
imaginative floral pattern. After several minutes of
conversation, she was free to join Max, who was sitting beside a chess table. He patted the footstool in
front of his chair, and she sank down facing him.

He reached out to take the white queen, twirling
the little carving in his hand. "Do you play?" he
asked.

"Only poorly, I fear."

"I shall have to see what I can do to brush up
your skills. You seem bright enough to understand
the game, so it must be that you have not had
enough opportunity to play."

Amity blushed at the compliment and vowed to
pay close attention to any instructions he should
give her. In truth she enjoyed the game, but her
governesses eschewed it as a male pastime, and she
had only found a few others in the neighborhood
who knew the rudiments of the game. Her eyes followed the movement of Max's hand as he returned
the queen to her square and lifted a knight, his
long fingers gently caressing the ivory figure. For
some unknown reason her face felt hot, and she
quickly shifted her eyes to the hands in her lap.

"Now, Amity," Max said, placing the chess piece
back on the board and taking a heartening sip of

his brandy. "What cockle-headed notion have you got that you must need rush into marriage?"

"Well to be perfectly honest, I should very much like to have a child. Someone of my own that I might love and cherish." Amity paused, looking up into Max's face to see if he understood her words. "And of course the babe would love me," she finished softly.

Max noticed that the clear blue eyes shone with particular brilliance as she spoke the last sentence. He was reminded again of her interchange with Cousin Hester earlier in the evening. His brows bunched over his forehead as he stared at the grave little figure across from him. Suddenly he thought he suspected the truth, and he reached out, cupping her chin in his hand.

"What was your mother like, Amity?" he asked, watching with pleasure the startled look at the abrupt change of subject. Her face was so expressive, shrouding few of her thoughts. He wondered if after a year in society, she would still be so trusting. He was surprised at the dreamy expression that flitted across her face and the faraway look in her eyes as she remembered her mother.

"She was glorious, Max," she whispered. "Her name was Divinia, and the fashionable set called her 'Goddess Divine.' She was petite, almost doll-like, with enormous periwinkle blue eyes and a soft pink complexion. Her hair was golden, as if the sun's rays were caught in each curl. Everything about her was beautiful."

"And did you love her a great deal?"

"I fear it was much like worship. She was everything I wanted to be," Amity admitted, her voice shaky with emotion. "I was a great disappointment to her."

Max stared down at the veil of tears that filled Amity's eyes and cursed under his breath. Remembering the scrawny child Amity had once been, he could only guess as to her mother's reactions, but he suspected from the girl's words that Divinia had not been pleased with her child's looks. Amity appeared to have no awareness of her own potential as far above the touch of most ordinarily pretty girls. Looking down at his ward, he caught a vulnerability beneath her smiling, sweet nature, a feeling that she was unlovely and that no one really loved her.

Max cursed himself for having neglected the child for so long. He wondered how lonely she had been on an isolated estate with no family to love her. He could not undo the damage he had done, but he could surely make up to her for all that she had missed. He would show her that her uncommon looks were to be applauded, not dismissed. He would be family for her, love her like a brother, and then she would blossom into the beauty he knew her to be. He leaned forward and pressed a gentle kiss to her soft, white forehead.

At the press of his lips Amity smiled in contentment and nestled her cheek into the cushion of his hand. "Then you will arrange for my marriage?"

"First things first," Max said, dropping his hand and reaching once more for the brandy snifter. "One needs to go slowly, my enthusiastic child. You must learn not to dash into a situation. I am relieved to note that you have lost the habit of knocking things over."

Amity laughed, remembering the first time he

had seen her. "It only seems to happen when I am exceedingly nervous. My last governess cautioned me to breathe deeply at every quarter hour, and then I would not be so prone to knock things about."

"Did it work?" Max asked.

"No," Amity said, her face an embarrassed grimace. "The first thing I hit was the clock, and then I never knew what time it was."

Max chuckled at her remark, but then his face shifted to more sober lines. "Perhaps you should strive to think a little before you leap into action. A lady who desires to be married needs to display qualities that will encourage the gentlemen to see her as the perfect wife. Dignity is the cornerstone for elegant behavior."

"Miss Endicott, my governess, would be delighted to hear you thus advise me," Amity said, wrinkling her nose at his words. She sighed in resignation and looked gravely up into Max's face. "I will try, sir, but there are so many temptations that I sometimes forget my good intentions."

"Well, my dear, both Cousin Hester and myself will be here to remind you of your obligations. Although you were not aware of my presence, I was witness to your arrival today."

Amity blushed at his pejorative tone. He patted her shoulder in a reassuring gesture, but she suspected she was in for a lecture. In her mind's eye she could picture Miss Endicott nodding smugly.

"I could hardly approve your arrival, since the entire operation lacked the proper dignity. You should have waited to accept the assistance of the footman in descending from the coach instead of scrambling out as though you had been catapulted."

"But I am neither old nor infirm to need such assistance," she argued. "It seems so silly."

"Rules of propriety are never silly," Max said dampeningly. "When you descended, your bonnet was askew and your hands were bare."

"I lost my mittens," Amity admitted. "I did not think anyone would notice."

"Whether someone will notice is beside the point. A lady is measured by the attention she pays to the details. It may seem like a small affectation, but people set great store by these very trivialities. Omissions of small points of etiquette are a signal that one's manners are merely superficial, not a part of one's character." Max's voice was encouraging as he continued, "Perhaps, if you have a penchant for losing something, you might consider carrying an extra for emergencies."

"I would probably have to carry a portmanteau, since I am constantly losing things," Amity muttered. She pushed at a lock of hair which had escaped from the ribbon when she bent her head and tucked it behind her ear.

"And never, Amity," Max's voice was stiff with disapproval, "I repeat, never are you to notice, let alone discuss with a servant, the, eh, personal habits of your dog. A lady is above the flesh."

"Life was very much simpler at Beech House."

"You will learn, my dear," Max said as he smiled kindly down at the girl. "Once you begin to think before you leap into action, things will become rather easier. In the meantime you must cultivate a more formal attitude toward the servants. You must not chatter with them as if they are your friends. They are here to serve you, not entertain you."

Amity had begun to believe that she might be able to learn the ways of the gently born, but had not considered she would be asked to make such a sacrifice. She had always had friends among the servants. At Beech House they were her only friends. She made no comment, but she resolved that she would concentrate on her other faults, and perhaps this one area might be overlooked. Raising her head, she smiled sheepishly at her guardian.

"I shall try to improve my behavior, Max. Truly I will."

"Good show," he said, grateful that she had listened so carefully to his criticisms. "I realize that you have had few examples to follow, but I hope when you meet Miss Waterston, you will consider her demeanor and pattern yourself after her. She has a delicacy of mind and grace of manner that is the essence of the refined gentlewoman."

Amity heard the note of approval in her guardian's voice and vowed to copy the behavior of Honoria to a nicety. She could tell by the expression on Max's face that she must be very special. She wondered if he were in love with her. And now that she was getting to know her guardian, she hoped that if he was, Honoria returned his regard in full measure. It would be most romantic if Max planned to marry. On that happy thought, she was eager to go to London and make the acquaintance of the fashionable Miss Waterston.

Chapter Four

"Come on, Muffin," Amity whispered, nudging the great shaggy animal off the satin love seat. "It's time for your walk."

Grabbing a handful of fur on his neck, she opened the door and peered into the empty hall. She tiptoed along the runner, the dog beside her, and slipped down the main staircase to the front door. She unlatched it and shoved Muffin out onto the front steps of the London town house, then closed the door quietly behind her. Breathing in the moist early morning air, she tied the ribbons on her bonnet and searched frantically in the pocket of her pelisse until she discovered her mittens. Pulling them on, she briskly started down the stairs. After an initial hesitancy Muffin shook his head and padded after her quickly disappearing figure.

Amity knew Max would be furious if he discovered her early morning adventures. Since their arrival in London, he had continually warned her about disgracing herself with unladylike behavior. She knew it was not proper to be out at such an hour and most especially without either a maid or a footman. However, she had found her entire life so confining that this bit of rebellion helped her immeasurably to get through the rest of each day. She walked the two blocks to the park, sighing in relief as she entered the gates.

She had discovered the little park on her second day in London, and it had become her private refuge. Used to the freedom of the country, she found the buildings and dirt of the city oppressive and needed her spirits renewed in this little plot of greenery.

Off the main paths, she felt safe from any unwanted eyes of the fashionable set. She walked slowly, letting Muffin poke and sniff as much as he wanted. Eventually she found a bench in the sun and sat down, calling softly to the dog. After taking one more investigative sniff of a particularly interesting clump of brush, he nestled contentedly at her feet.

Untying the ribbons on her bonnet, Amity pulled off the hat and placed it beside her. She turned her face up to the sun, her eyes closed as her skin soaked in the heat. It was a perfect day, and she should have felt a well of excitement for all that had happened in the last month. But her come-out ball was this evening, and just the thought of it sent her stomach plummeting to her toes.

"Oh, Muffin, I've been such a fool," Amity moaned. The dog raised his shaggy head and stared at her with soulful eyes. She reached down and stroked his soft fur, and he pressed his head against her knee, letting it slide down until it rested on her foot. "It was my pride that done me in, old sport."

For a moment a smile trembled on her lips at her

joking tone, but then her eyes filled with tears. How was she ever going to get through this evening? Her dress had arrived yesterday, and it was a total disaster; she would be a total disaster. She had been so foolish in her pride, and now she would pay the price for her vanity. But more than her disappointment over the dress was her awareness of Honoria's betrayal. As unsophisticated as she was, even she had to acknowledge that the woman she thought had befriended her had indeed betrayed her trust.

Muffin snuffled in his sleep, and Amity was reminded of her one loyal friend. She reached into her reticule and pulled out a lacy handkerchief. She blew her nose and wiped her eyes, admonishing herself for giving in to such a degree. After all, it was her own fault.

Amity had liked Honoria when she first met her. The very fashionable Miss Waterston was five years older with a social manner that Amity envied. Beside the elegant perfection of the blond woman, she had felt like the veriest gawk, but Max's special lady friend had been charming to her, taking her shopping, and praising her for her fashion sense. Amity had been dazzled by the endless bolts of materials and trimmings at the mantua maker. She had been flattered when Honoria asked her opinion on all the selections. At first she had been hesitant, but under the older woman's praise, she gained confidence in her choices. Soon she was giving her imagination full rein, choosing dresses that she had dreamed about over the bleak years at Beech House.

It was only in the last week that Amity first suspected that everything was not what it should be. Madame Bertoldi, the modiste Honoria had brought her to, had become more tight-lipped as the fittings continued. It was apparent to Amity that the woman was not happy with the dresses, but each time she opened her mouth to speak, Honoria interrupted sharply. When Amity questioned Honoria, she laughed off her concerns, saying foreigners always were moody.

Yesterday when the ball gown arrived, Amity had been filled with excitement. Since her arrival in London, she had become more aware of fashions and dreamed about the thrill of being dressed properly. She could not wait another moment to see the results of her endless shopping. Hurrying to her room, she had locked the door and folded back the tissue around the dress. The dress was just as she had pictured it, and she sighed with happiness. Slipping out of her morning gown, she gingerly pulled the dress over her head. Her hands shook as she tied the sash beneath her breasts and crossed the room until she stood in front of the cheval glass. Slowly she raised her eyes.

A cry of disappointment came to her lips, but she bit it back as she stared at the dreadful vision in the mirror. The beautiful dress looked ludicrous. Her shoulders slumped and she covered her eyes, wanting nothing more than to run away back to Beech House. She gave in to the feeling of self-pity for only a few minutes before her more practical sense came to her aid. Taking her hands away from her eyes, she stared into the mirror trying to look objectively at the dress.

The dress itself was a beautiful creation. It was

white muslin, which Honoria had told her was de rigueur for a debutante. The bodice was tucked and pleated down to the pink sash tied beneath her breasts. The skirt had wide, stiffly pleated ruffles which were caught up around the edge with bright pink bows to show off the shell pink underskirt. Honoria had advised that the sleeves be puffed at the shoulder and had suggested Amity might like the bows repeated on the material covering her arms down to her wrists. The dress was exactly like the one Amity and Honoria had designed.

The problem was that the gown would have looked beautiful on Honoria's petite figure. On Amity the dress accentuated her height and was much too fussy for her larger figure. Perhaps it might not have been so awful, but the bright color of the pink sash and bows clashed with her hair, setting her teeth on edge. Closing her eyes, Amity remembered Honoria holding the pink satin material against her cheek.

"This color truly brings out the highlights in your hair, my dear." Honoria's voice echoed in Amity's head. "And it does wonders for your skin tones."

Sitting on the bench in the park, Amity bowed her head, embarrassed that she had been so easily gulled. She did not understand why Honoria had let her choose her own wardrobe when her unsophisticated choices had been so wrong. She had been betrayed by her own foolish pride and the older woman who she thought was standing as friend. She still found it hard to believe that Honoria would be so cruel as to make her a laughingstock, but if she wore the dress this evening, Amity knew that would be the result.

Part of Amity's anguish was in knowing that she would disappoint Max. Her guardian had been wonderful to her, and she would repay him by appearing like the veriest country bumpkin. She wanted nothing so much as to throw herself on his chest and cry out all her woes, but that was an impossibility. It was apparent from the beginning that Honoria had a special position in Max's life. There was a proprietary air about the woman when she spoke of him that indicated to Amity that their relationship was not one of mere friendship. In the last few days Honoria had hinted that Max was near to declaring himself, and that had destroyed any thought of Amity's that she might confide her troubles to him.

How could Amity tell Max that the woman he loved had purposely set out to ruin his ward's chances in society? She had trusted Honoria and had not looked beyond the woman's words to the character beneath. It was only lately that she had begun to question Honoria's motives, but she had ignored the inconsistencies since Max thought so highly of the woman. Could Max not see beyond the woman's beautiful facade? And if he couldn't, it was not up to Amity to destroy his illusions.

For some reason Honoria had taken her in dislike, but Amity could not wholly blame the woman. She had been far too trusting. Now she understood why Madame Bertoldi had been so unsettled. The Frenchwoman knew that Amity's choices were wrong, but had been afraid of losing Honoria's custom by arguing. In the light of this discovery, Amity suspected that the other garments in her wardrobe also would be wrong for her. A spurt of anger forced her head up, and she glared sightlessly at the cinder path.

"I shan't be a spineless doll, Muffin," she said with decision. The dog raised his head, cocking his ears as she reached down to scratch him. "I have been far too trusting. For some reason Honoria has taken me in dislike, but now that I am aware of the situation, I should be able to salvage something. Tomorrow I shall go back to Madame Bertoldi without Honoria and see what we can do to ensure that the rest of my wardrobe is suitable. For tonight I shall just hold my head up and smile."

Standing up, Amity brushed down her skirts and squared her shoulders. She picked up her bonnet, plopped it on her head, and tied the ribbons. Having made a decision, she was determined to enjoy the rest of her morning stroll. Muffin lumbered to his feet, staring around at the park as though surprised to be there. Amity strolled aimlessly down the path, stopping occasionally to peer more closely at the foliage along the way. The path turned sharply to the right, and just before she rounded the corner, Amity clearly heard the sound of crying. She stopped, trying to locate the sound, but Muffin bounded ahead and disappeared from sight. A shrill screech was choked off, and Amity dashed around the corner.

A girl her own age was pressed against a bench, cowering away from Muffin. A handkerchief was clutched in her hand, which she waved in front of the dog as though warding off evil. Amity hurried forward and grabbed a handful of fur, then extended her hand to reassure the girl.

"He's really not fearsome," she said. "Come on, you great looby. You're frightening the lady."

Pulling Amity along, Muffin shambled forward until his nose was pressed against the black dress of the terrified girl. He raised his shaggy head, staring at her with his great soulful eyes, then lifted one hairy paw and placed it gently in her lap. The girl hiccupped once, raised her eyes to Amity's encouraging face, then stared down at the dog. After a moment's hesitation she lifted the hand holding the handkerchief and tentatively stroked the hair on his back.

"I'm sorry I screamed, miss. He's really a sweet old thing." Across the dog's back the girl gave a watery smile to Amity.

Amity took in the reddened eyes and tear tracks on the girl's face and moved closer. Since she had just been feeling so desperate herself, she recognized the signs in the other girl. Pretending to notice nothing amiss, she sat down on the other end of the bench.

"This is Muffin. I'm ever so sorry he frightened you. Normally we don't see anyone at this time of the morning." Amity bent her head, busily patting the dog's back as the girl scrubbed surreptitiously at her tearstained cheeks.

"I expect it was the surprise," the girl said shyly. "When I set down there was not many jaunting around."

"Am I intruding?" Amity asked. "I didn't mean to be rude."

"No, please don't go," the girl said, lifting her hand as though to hold Amity in place. "I was sunk in a fit of the sullens as me mum used to say, and that will never do. I would truly enjoy talking to someone."

"It's so nice to have a friend to talk to," Amity admitted. Smiling she introduced herself. "Muffin and I are new to London, and we have made no particular friends. Sometimes it is very lonely."

The girl took the extended hand and bobbed her head as though making a curtsy. "I am Betta Twidleigh. I'm most pleased to meet you." She then reached for the paw in her lap and shook it, Muffin responded by opening his mouth and yawning hugely.

Both girls giggled as the dog slumped at their feet, sprawling contentedly on the sun-warmed grass. For several minutes they sat contentedly on the bench, then Amity coughed in embarrassment.

"I know it is the height of rudeness to intrude on your thoughts, but sometimes a problem shared is less in weight." Amity flushed as Betta scanned her face, but the girl did not seem insulted, only nodded her head in agreement.

"I am a thief," the girl blurted out as if the words were torn from her. At Amity's gasp of surprise she added, "At least my mistress accused me of stealing. But truly I did not take the bracelet."

"My apologies, Betta, for insulting you with such missish behavior, but it was the surprise of your words," Amity said.

"It's of no mind, Miss Amity. I'd be happy to explain if you would care to listen." At Amity's quick nod, she continued, "I was abigail to Mistress Euphemia Teasdale. Her husband is in banking, and she felt her social position required a body servant.

I worked for her for two years. She was not too difficult a mistress.''

Betta's brief words gave Amity a picture of a bleak existence in the household of a nouveau riche cit. Now that she had a chance to look more carefully, she could see that Betta was a well-spoken servant with the clean look of a country girl. She had a long face, not singularly pretty but set off by warm brown eyes. Her black bombazine dress was neat, and her brown hair was tucked beneath a spotless mobcap. There was a crisp, no-nonsense air about the girl that Amity liked.

"Two days ago Mistress Teasdale attended a party without her husband. I had it from the parlor maid, who is stepping out with the coachman, that it was a gambling party." Betta made a moue of disapproval, sighed, and then continued with her story. "She was very late in getting home and seemed truly overset. I helped her into her night things, put away her jewelry and then, since she seemed so distraught, brought her a cup of warm milk. She dismissed me immediately, and I hurried to bed, knowing I would have to be up in less than five hours."

Betta paused and stared blindly at the bushes on the far side of the path. Her forehead was lined in puzzlement, and her fingers pulled at the handkerchief in her lap. For a moment her chin quivered, and Amity leaned forward and placed her own hand on top of the girl's in encouragement.

"Yesterday I was woken with a powerful commotion. Sarah, the cook, was shaking me and told me the mistress was screaming her head off. I hurried into my clothes and ran to her room only to see her raise her finger to point at me in fury." Betta's face whitened at the memory of the terrible scene, and she squeezed Amity's hand for courage. "Banker Teasdale was there, and Mistress Teasdale was sobbing and tearing her hair. She called me terrible names and accused me of stealing her diamond bracelet."

"That is the outside of enough!" Amity declared, furious at the injustice done to her new friend. "Surely you explained you had not done any such thing."

Betta smiled at the girl's immediate defense. "I tried to, but she would not listen. She kept calling me a sly, deceitful girl and turned me out without a letter of recommendation."

"The ungrateful woman!" Amity jumped to her feet in her agitation. Having been involved in the running of Beech House, she was well aware of the impossibility of finding a job without a character. Whirling around, she faced Betta, glaring fiercely at the girl. "And I hope you told her so."

For the first time since they began talking, Betta's face broke into a genuine smile of enjoyment. She began to laugh until tears stood in her eyes, while Amity continued to stare down at her. Finally she too realized the humor in the situation and sat back down, joining the other girl in laughter.

Finally Betta wiped her streaming eyes. "With your red hair and your flashing eyes, you reminded me of an angry cock me mum used to keep."

"What happened to him?"

"We ate him."

At the words the girls once more fell into laughter. Muffin raised his head, staring at them through sleepy eyes, then snuffling in disgust, he slumped back on the grass.

"You have made me feel so much better," Betta said, patting Amity's arm when she could control her giggles.

"I'm glad for that," Amity said. "But what do you suppose did happen to the bracelet?"

Betta's long face turned serious. "I have thought and thought, and finally I think I have discovered the answer. I do not recall seeing the bracelet when I put away the jewelry. I think Mistress Teasdale wagered the bracelet at the gambling party. As I mentioned earlier, she was very agitated when she returned. She kept wringing her hands and staring at the door connecting to her husband's suite of rooms. I think she decided to claim it was stolen rather than admit she had lost it gambling."

"What will you do now, Betta?" Amity asked.

"I spent the rest of yesterday going to the employment agencies, but without a letter I have little hope of securing a position."

Once more her chin began to tremble, and Amity's heart went out to the girl. Since her arrival in London, she had seen many areas of the city where the poor subsisted in filth and squalor. The thought that the neat little figure beside her should be reduced to such circumstances forced her to take charge.

"Then you shall come and be my abigail," she said.

"You're bamming me," Betta blurted out in astonishment.

"Truly I'm not," Amity said. Her voice was serious as she turned to the girl. "I have a need for a new abigail. Pauline has been taking care of me, but she doesn't half like the job."

"Are you that sorry a mistress?" Betta asked.

"I will admit that I am ever so crabby in the morning, but it is not for that Pauline wants to return to the kitchens. She is walking out with one of the footmen, and she says she never gets a chance to see him now that she spends so much time in my room. When she was a parlor maid, she could slip off to the kitchen whenever he was near." The more Amity thought about the idea of Betta as her abigail, the more enthusiastic she became. "There really is not a lot to do for me, and I would be ever so pleased to have someone I could talk to."

Betta's face was expressionless as her huge eyes scanned Amity. It was evident the girl was sincere, and she truly was in desperate straits, but more than that, there was an appeal behind the words, which inclined Betta to accept the position without question. Slowly her wide mouth pulled in a grin, and she nodded her head in agreement.

"You are quite the answer to my prayers, Betta," Amity said, quickly hugging the girl. "I have made a sad muddle of my life since I came to London."

Briefly Amity explained about Honoria and the folly of her wardrobe while Betta listened wide-eyed. Although Amity was mystified by the betrayal, the servant had little difficulty guessing that it was a simple matter of jealousy. She had already taken in the potential beauty of her new mistress and could well imagine the other young lady feeling threatened. She kept her opinion to herself, recognizing a sweet naïveté in Amity that she had no desire to despoil. There was time enough for her mistress to discover the many evils in the world.

"Will your guardian approve of your choice?" Betta asked hesitantly.

"He will be so busy with the details for the ball this evening that he will agree to anything." Amity chuckled. "He's been wearing a black scowl since the caterers and florists arrived, and yesterday in desperation, he abandoned the house for the sanctity of his club. Lady Grassmere is little help, and although I have offered to be of assistance, the butler and the housekeeper have things well in train."

Reminded of the ball, Amity shivered as she thought about the dress she must wear tonight. As if they had been friends for many years, Betta assured her that between the two of them they ought to be able to figure out something to make the gown appear more suitable. Perhaps, the dress might not be such a disaster after all. Much in charity with each other, the girls awakened the dog and hurried back to the town house. Putnam awaited her arrival and with a cautionary air warned her that Lord Max was awaiting her in the library. Amity introduced Betta and turned her new abigail over to the butler, then straightening her bonnet and brushing out her skirts, she hurried up the stairs and along the hall to the library. Opening the door quietly, she peeped around the edge of the door.

The library was her favorite room in the town

house. It was a large room with shelves of books on three sides, rising to the painted representations of the constellations on the ornate ceiling. The fourth wall held a charming window seat within the bow window and looked out on the walled garden with the mews behind. Max was seated in a deep leather chair behind an enormous mahogany desk. As if he sensed her presence, his head jerked up, and he pierced her with his sharp green gaze.

"Devil take it, Amity! Where have you been?" Max shouted.

"I—I," she stammered in surprise at her guardian's furious expression.

"Don't just stand there like some gapeworm," he snapped. "What exactly have you to say for yourself? It is my understanding that you and that ill-kempt beast of yours were gallivanting around town with no attendants. May I remind you that in London it takes little to give the old tabbies a disgust of you. Your reputation could be in shreds after such an escapade."

"I'm sorry, Max, but . . ." Amity began only to be cut off by her guardian.

"You are a hurly-burly girl. Just look at you. Your hair is flying about your face like some tousled baggage."

Max was astounded at the extent of his anger. He had sent for her after breakfast and was stunned to discover that she was nowhere to be found. He had been pacing the library ever since, all too aware of the dangers that could befall an innocent young girl, and now she had the unmitigated gall to bounce into the room, cheeks flushed and hair spilling around her face in riotous curls like a veritable hoyden. The wide clear blue of her eyes held a wounded look that only exacerbated his annoyance. He glared at her, and she had the grace to flush and dip her head in embarrassment.

"Have you any excuse for such behavior?" Max asked, his voice a thin stream of ice.

Quickly Amity peeked through her lowered lashes. Although he was still angry, the worst of his temper seemed to have been expelled. Perhaps this was not the best of times to approach the subject of her abigail, but she suspected that he had given her enough of an opening that she could not afford to let it pass.

"I realize, sir, that my behavior appears unseemly, but I was on a particular errand this morning. You see, I have need of a new abigail," she ventured.

"You went out on the street to find a servant." The words were laced with sarcasm, and Amity could see the muscles in his jaw tighten in returning anger.

"Naturally not, milord. Honoria told me there were agencies that handled the employment of servants."

Amity did not feel that the mention of the woman's name was unfair. She did recall that they had spoken of various household problems, and it was altogether possible that their discussion had included the hiring of servants. In any event, she hoped Max would not question her too closely. She could see that the mention of the socially correct Miss Waterston did much to alleviate her guardian's temper. For the first time that day, Amity felt grateful to Honoria.

"But, my girl, the butler should have applied to the agency."

Max sat down behind his desk, indicating that Amity should sit across from him. He rubbed a hand over his forehead, wondering how many other things he had failed to warn the impetuous child about. She had no conception of the dangers that lurked about the London streets. He stared into her clear blue eyes and wondered what it must be like to be so trusting. On the one hand he wanted to warn her, but in the same breath he did not want to do anything to spoil her view of the world. He must protect her until he found a suitable party, one he could entrust the girl to without fear she would come to harm.

"Now, Amity, perhaps you would be good enough to explain about the abigail."

Briefly she outlined her need for an abigail, and her success in discovering one she thought quite suitable. She tried to stick as closely to the truth as she could and must have succeeded, for at the end Max nodded his agreement.

"Kennicut's Employment Register is quite reputable. And this Betta came highly recommended?" Max asked.

"She had been abigail to a banker's wife for several years," Amity evaded, then hurried on before he could question her further. "But more to the point, sir, the girl is well-spoken and very eager to please. I liked her mightily."

"I wish you had come to me before you plunged into such a situation. However, I do applaud your attempt to handle your own affairs," Max said, wishing to be fair. He was unwilling to capitulate entirely to Amity's outrageous adventure. She needed to learn that there was a proper way to do things. "My suggestion would be to try her for the week. If at the end of that time, we are *both*"—he stressed the word—"satisfied, she will remain."

Amity's face beamed with pleasure as she leaped up, clapping her hands in delight. Throwing a kiss to her bemused guardian, she scampered out of the room. Max remained seated, curiously touched by the joy his ward found in such small things. He was sorry now that he had shouted at her. His hand reached inside his coat, and he extracted a velvet box which he laid on the desk. His long fingers tapped on the lid, and he pictured the expression on Amity's face when he presented her with the string of pearls.

He had intended she wear them on this special evening. Originally he had toyed with the idea of making Amity's debut an occasion of double celebration by announcing his betrothal to Honoria. He had chided himself for his failure to declare his intentions to Miss Waterston, but he found he was loath to commit himself. It was not that he had changed his mind. Honoria was everything he wanted in a bride. His mind had been occupied with the problem of Amity, and he had not had the opportunity to settle his own affairs. Once his ward was successfully launched, he would speak to Honoria about their own relationship.

Besides, this evening should be a singular celebration for Amity. He was exceedingly pleased with how well she had adapted to her new life. He could see that once he had explained the qualities that she must aspire to, the girl had striven to become more ladylike.

Dealing with his ward was no different from dealing with any other woman. One needed only to impress on the girl that things must be done properly, in an ordered fashion. Once she gave up her hoydenish ways, she would make the perfect wife for any man. Her bursts of enthusiasm and rash behavior would soon vanish, and her behavior would be a model of decorum. He scratched his chin, wondering why the picture of Amity as the soul of docility should sit so ill on his mind.

Chapter Five

"It's worse than I remember." Amity moaned and her shoulders slumped as she looked into the mirror.

"I'll admit it doesn't do you a treat. Lud, I wish me mum were here. She was wizard with a needle." Betta circled behind her mistress, eyeing the dress from every angle. Her long nose was wrinkled as she debated what to do for the best. "I thought perhaps with your hair up in curls one wouldn't notice the dress. Ain't much of an improvement."

Amity stared wistfully at the intricate shower of ringlets and had to agree with her friend's opinion. The ornate arrangement of curls only emphasized the fussiness of the dress. They had already spent several hours trying different hairstyles, but none of them had diminished the effect of the gown. She was doomed.

At the light scratching on the hall door, the girls froze and exchanged apprehensive glances. Moments later the sound was repeated with a decided impatience to the summons. Shrugging in resignation, Amity waved her hand to Betta, who opened the door. Much to their surprise it was Max, who stood transfixed in the doorway.

"Good Lord, Amity! What is that?"

"It's my gown for this evening." Amity raised her chin, forced by pride to defend the much maligned dress.

"Devil, you say!" Max blurted out, then clamped his mouth shut when he saw the look of misery on the girl's face. With only a momentary hesitation, he closed the door and strode into the center of the room. "Turn around, Amity. I wish to be privy to the sensational features of your gown."

Cheeks flushed in embarrassment, Amity slowly turned in a circle, coming to a stop facing him. Her head was bent because she had little desire to see the contempt in his eyes for her ludicrous costume.

Max felt as though he had taken a blow to his rib cage. How was it possible that the girl was wearing a dress that was so patently wrong for her? Honoria would never have permitted her to make such a choice. The dress was clearly more in Honoria's style than Amity's, but he still did not understand how such a mistake could have been made. But more to the point, what on earth were they to do at this late hour?

"I'm dreadfully sorry, Max," Amity said in a strained voice.

"Enough said, child. The dress is not suited to you, but since our guests will be arriving in another few hours, we will have to put our heads together to see what we might contrive."

The relief on Amity's upturned face sent a jolt of sensation much like a pain slicing through Max's chest. He should be angry that the girl had obviously made a hash of things, but she looked so woebegone that he did not have the heart to lecture her. Later there would be time for recriminations; now there was work to be done if they were not all to land in the soup. Folding his arms over his chest, Max stared at the gown through narrowed eyes.

"Turn again so I may see the back." He cocked his head to the side, then raised his hand to pull at his lower lip. "You. Girl," he said turning to the young abigail, who was wringing her hands in her apron. "Come over here."

"Aye, sir," Betta said, her voice shaking with nervousness. She bobbed a curtsy, standing with eyes lowered in front of Lord Kampford.

Max liked the look of the neat little figure. She was of an age with his ward, and her plain face and clean appearance was a far cry from the slovenly servants he had seen in other houses. Although reluctant to give full approval to Amity's selection, he was in general pleased with the girl. "Your name?"

"Betta, milord," she said, bobbing another curtsy.

"Can you sew, Betta?" he asked.

"Only the most basic stitches."

"It'll do. For a start, cut off that sash and every one of those ever-so-charming bows."

Then, ignoring the girls, he stalked to the wardrobe and threw open the doors. He eyed the contents, occasionally extending a hand to finger a material, then shaking his head in rejection. Finally he extracted a dress of soft wool, nodding in approval of the blues and greens of the plaid. He remembered the night Amity had arrived at Edgeworth. She had worn the dress to dinner, and he

remembered how startled he had been at the transformation of the gawky child into such an exotic
creature. He turned to stare thoughtfully at Amity,
and a small grin tugged at the corner of his mouth.

Dress in hand, he picked up a dainty lilac satin
side chair and moved over closer to the girls. Amity's cheeks were flushed, and she sent him a wa-
vering smile as he turned the chair around so he
could sit with his arms braced across the back. The
floor was littered with the bilious pink bows, and
he winked at his ward as the final one trembled at
her shoulder, then fluttered down to the carpet.

"Now, *mes enfants*, I will give you an important
piece of advice," Max said, tenting his fingers and
pointing at the two startled girls. "Never take half
measures. Society loves the outrageous. They are
jaded souls prepared to accept the most outlandish
of stories."

He outlined his plan for the gown, grinning at
the look of amazement on the girls' faces. Once they
understood what was required, they exchanged
glances and then burst into laughter, while Max
looked on in approval.

"Are ye up to the challenge, me hearties?"

"Aye, sir," Amity answered, while Betta nodded
in agreement.

"Then I shall up anchor, leaving you to the drudge
work."

Without a backward glance Max crossed to the
door, leaving behind him a flurry of activity. He
smiled as he listened to the soft voices, slightly
shrill with excitement and shared laughter. He
sauntered down the hall to his rooms hoping that

the sheer audacity of their project might be rewarded.

"You look exceedingly elegant this evening, cousin," Max said, bowing to cover a grin as Lady Grassmere edged cautiously into the main salon.

Cousin Hester was as usual in gray, the dress hardly varying in style from the others in her wardrobe. The only addition to indicate the importance of the occasion was the necklace of diamonds that glittered at her neck. She breathlessly whispered a greeting, then sank gratefully onto the settee, folding her hands primly in her lap.

Max tried not to fidget, but was filled with a restlessness as the hour for the guests' arrival drew near. He had done what he could to salvage the situation, and now he must rely on Amity for the rest. His shoulders tensed at the sound of footsteps crossing the marble hall. The doors swung open on well-oiled hinges, and his eyes widened as his ward entered the room, stopping just inside the doorway.

Amity resembled the ancient warrior goddess he had pictured the night she arrived at Edgeworth. It was difficult to recall the appalling gown in the face of its transformation. The sleeves were still puffed, but the material swathing her arms had been removed, replaced by long white gloves. The stiffly pleated ruffle had been torn from the bottom of the overskirt, and the muslin remaining was frayed like the tatters on a pauper. Now that all of the bright pink bows were gone, the pink underskirt seemed softer, more nearly peach in tone. The plaid material had been cut and resewn as a long sash, falling from one shoulder to cross her bosom where it was attached at the waist with a round, filigree silver ornament. Without all the ruffles and bows, the simple style of the gown was well suited to the tall, red-haired girl.

Raising his eyes to her face, Max felt a tightening in his chest at the look of pride on his ward's face. Her clear blue eyes shimmered like the water in a Scottish loch. Her hair had been combed out and was brushed to a burnished ripple of curls that hung down her back to her waist. She wore no jewelry, only a circle of small, white flowers crowned her head.

"Oh my word, child," cousin Hester cried, so unsettled that her voice rose to a shrill screech. "What sort of May game are you playing at?"

"Fustian, cousin," Max said, stepping forward to take Amity's hand and draw her farther into the room. "Surely you have seen the traditional regalia for a Scottish maiden."

"Scottish?" Hester's eyes goggled as they swung between her cousin and his ward.

"It was demmed clever of Amity to remind us of her illustrious heritage on such an occasion."

Amity's mouth trembled with the effort it took not to laugh at Max's drawled tone. Entering eagerly into the affair, she pursed her mouth and commented in injured tones. "Everything is near perfect, Lady Grassmere, except that Max would not permit me to wear the knife at my belt."

"Knife?" Hester uttered weakly, groping in her reticule for her ever present bottle of salts.

"Naughty, puss," Max hissed, then raised his voice to a bright, chivying tone. "Never say, Cousin Hester, that you have forgotten the traditions of the Frasers of Scotland. Amity does exceedingly well to bring honor to her ancestors." Knowing he was striking at one of his cousin's pet animadversions, he added, "Young girls nowadays rarely applaud the past, but are more interested in the fashions and etiquette of a more modern world."

Like a fish, Hester leaped at the bait. "Our Amity is not light-minded like most young girls," she whispered.

Amity bit the inside of her cheek so as not to go off in whoops, since Lady Grassmere had been chiding her continually for her impetuous behavior, which she considered quite scatterbrained. She lowered her eyes modestly, knowing that if her gaze crossed Max's, she would ruin herself in the eyes of her chaperon.

"How perceptive you are, cousin," Max said. His voice had a choked quality, but after clearing his throat, he was able to continue. "Perhaps I might remind you of the significance of Amity's costume in the event some of our guests should not be *epris* of Scottish traditions. The sash is naturally the tartan of her family's clan. As my ward so delightfully mentioned, owing to the sensibilities of some of our gently reared ladies, the ancestral dagger has been replaced by a broach of heraldic design."

"Very tasteful, Maxwell," Hester simpered.

"Why, thank you, cousin." He spoke more loudly than usual to cover the chortle of laughter that slipped from his ward's stiffly smiling lips.

"And the torn skirts?" Hester asked, leaning forward in her interest.

Max looked momentarily blank, and there was

an uneasy silence for several moments before Amity stepped quickly into the breach.

"How clever of you to notice, Lady Grassmere," she said, trying to remember Max's original plan. "The ragged edges are merely symbolic."

"Symbolic of what, dear child?" Hester said. "This is all so exciting you see. I must admit I know very little of Scottish customs, but I should imagine some equally unenlightened will ask."

"One might have assumed as much," Amity said, casting her eyes to the ceiling for inspiration. "Well it indicates, that is, it is symbolic of, eh, poverty. Ah yes, poverty."

"Yes?" the old lady asked.

"Do go on, Amity. No need to be missish in the face of Cousin Hester's curiosity," Max said, leaning negligently against the side of a glass-fronted bookcase, arms folded across his chest, and his head cocked to the side in great interest. His ward narrowed her eyes, and he suspected for his own peace of mind that in future he would be wiser not to goad her.

Amity chuckled at the wary expression that crossed Max's face, and she determined to give a good accounting of herself. She was so concentrated on impressing her guardian with her inventiveness that she forgot the presence of Lady Grassmere.

"My family dates back many centuries and over the years many customs have changed, but always there is an echo of the old days. The laird called all the clan together when his daughter came of age. For days they celebrated with fairs and games and, uh, hunting," Amity invented. Her eyes flashed as she became caught up in her own narrative. "At midnight the entire clan would stand in a circle, and the proud father would lead his daughter to the center. Flagons of wine would be raised in a toast to the marriageable girl. Then, in order to prove that she was a maiden of exceptional beauty, he would rend her garments until she stood before the clan in nothing except the veil of her hair."

As Lady Grassmere took in the significance of the girl's words, her wrinkled cheeks flamed with color, then whitened to an ashy pallor. Amity was immediately contrite, dismayed that her need to revenge herself on Max had led her to so distress the older woman. She ran forward and dropped to her knees before Lady Grassmere.

"I beg your pardon for my ill-considered words, milady. I have a wicked tongue and should be beaten for my remarks."

The tone of sincerity in the girl's voice did much to soothe the older woman's sense of ill-usage. Her face returned to a more normal color, and she patted Amity's cheek to indicate she appreciated the girl's concern.

"My apologies for my tasteless joke, Lady Grassmere. It was nothing but a bold fiction. In actual fact the torn skirts indicate that a young girl should not be judged by her wealth but the sweetness and generosity of her nature."

"That is decidedly charming," Cousin Hester said in relief. "Sentiments I can wholeheartedly approve. Now stand up and turn around so that I might see the full effect."

Amity did as requested and earned a wink of encouragement from Max, who also was feeling

slightly ashamed of his outrageous behavior. He
had been much touched by his ward's immediate
awareness that she had gone too far. He had noticed that despite Cousin Hester's fluttery ways
and old-fashioned ideas, Amity never gave her
anything but the utmost respect. Her laughter
earlier had not been at the expense of the old
lady, but rather her enjoyment of the jest. There
was much to be lauded about the girl, despite her
impetuous nature. Very definitely a ward to be
proud of.

As the sounds of arrival echoed from the hall,
Max gathered Amity and Lady Grassmere to formally receive their guests.

"Egad, Honoria, whatever are you about with
such a paltry toilette?" Percy Waterston asked,
raising his quizzing glass to stare at his sister.

"Shut up, you ninny," Honoria hissed, brushing
out the wrinkles in her skirt. "I merely wanted a
simpler ensemble tonight."

"Simple, ma dear," Percy drawled. "It verges on
the bucolic."

Honoria wore a gown of heavy blue silk that was
patterned in the Grecian style. The classic design
did little to enhance her short, rounded figure. It
had always been her custom to wear filmy materials that floated around her to emphasize her petite-
ness. Aware at twenty-six that she was no longer a
debutante, she chose dresses with a youthful pret-
tiness and was partial to ruffles and bows.

"Don't be nasty or I shan't loan you another cent,
and you'll be forced to go to the moneylenders," she
snapped.

Honoria's voice was shrill, since she did not feel she was at her best in such a plain, unadorned gown. When she had originally thought of the idea for Amity's dress, she had imagined that the simplicity of her own apparel would further emphasize the gaucheness of the young girl. Now she was not so sure.

"Don't dawdle, Percy," she said, digging her sharp nails into the satin sleeve covering his arm.

"We certainly are in a wretched mood tonight." Percy led her toward the staircase, nodding graciously to several acquaintances. "I can see nursemaiding the little ward has put you quite out of temper. I myself am most anxious to meet the delightful Miss Fraser. One senses the unleashed talons that are ruining my jacket are intended instead for the little deb, *n'est pas*?"

"Don't be boring, brother dear." Her voice was carefully apathetic to indicate her disinterest, but her eyes flashed angrily for a moment much to Percy's amusement. "I have quite enjoyed jaunting about town with the girl. She's been bowled over by my offer of friendship since she knows no one else in town. But two weeks of ingenuous enthusiasm is more than I can abide. Besides I have nothing in common with the chit."

"Nothing but Max" came the acid retort.

Honoria dug her nails into her brother's arm, all the time smiling graciously. It was a smile that never reached her eyes. "It is time and enough to be about my own affairs. I am positive Max is on the brink of making me an offer, and if you know what's good for you, you'll do what you can to encourage the match. It would be a pity if the rest of the ton discovered that your pockets were to let."

"Too cruel, sister mine. If I weren't in such desperate straits, I would let Max truly discover what sort of woman he is about to marry."

Percy clenched his teeth, knowing that he could never risk such a satisfying revenge. It was to his best interest that Honoria marry Max. Unlimited advantages would be available through his connection to Lord Kampford. The duns would cease hounding him; the opera dancers would once more seek his patronage. His sister's gasp brought him back to the reality of the moment, and he turned to see a false smile of greeting stretched across her face.

Amity had been waiting for the arrival of Honoria and had not missed the momentary shock as the woman took in her improvised gown. She extended her gloved hand in a graceful, almost regal gesture as the woman approached.

"At last, Honoria, I have been breathless for your arrival," Amity said, adopting the woman's artificially bored tones.

"La, sweet child, how gracious you are this evening." Honoria smiled although her pale blue eyes were narrowed like a cat's. "You look quite *ravissant.*"

"Thank you for your kind words," Amity said. She was surprised that she did not feel as awkward as usual beside the elegant Miss Waterston. On closer observation she realized that Honoria did not look as striking as she had expected. She had always been envious of the breathtaking ensembles the woman wore, but this evening her gown was quite plain. Perhaps she had not wanted to steal any of Amity's attention, and in her envy Amity had done the woman an injustice by suspecting her of deliberately sabotaging her wardrobe.

"How sweet to wear your hair au naturel, just as if you knew nothing about the current mode."

Honoria's sugary words dispelled any doubt for Amity of the woman's goodwill. They were clearly at daggers drawn. She smiled stiffly, speaking carefully for the benefit of her guardian. "I appreciate such a compliment from someone of your vast experience."

Honoria's eyes flashed dangerously, but without another word she turned to Max, her eyelashes fluttering as she tapped him coyly on the arm with her fan. "And you, good sir, look exceedingly handsome this evening."

Amity wanted nothing more than to listen to the exchange between Honoria and her guardian, but, mindful of her social duties, turned to the elegant dandy who was waiting to be received. When she realized he was Honoria's brother, her smile of welcome faltered.

"No need to fear, my pet," Percy drawled. "I can see now why my sister has been in such a state. I have nothing but admiration for anyone who can so quickly put Honoria out of countenance."

Amity giggled as he gave her an extravagant leg. Seeing the response in his twinkling eyes, she relaxed her guard and spoke more easily to him. "I did not know Honoria had a brother."

"It is a fact that she would just as soon forget," he said, grimacing in the direction of his sister. "Perhaps you might save me a dance later, and I can tell you the sad story of my life. It is very droll, my angel."

Percy turned to speak to Max, and Amity awaited the next introduction from Lady Grassmere. She was impressed with her chaperon's grasp of names and titles. The little woman never hesitated, her voice a sibilant whisper as she smiled a greeting to each newcomer. Soon the majority of the guests had arrived, and Max indicated that it was time to open the ball.

For Amity the entire evening whirled together in a kaleidoscope of colors and scenes. The rich satins and silks, the glitter of diamonds and gems too numerous to recall, the glorious music all joined together in her mind, a memory she would hold dear all the days of her life. But the moments most precious to her were the ones when Max danced with her. She could see in his face that he was proud of her, and her heart swelled with gratitude that it was so. There was nothing she wanted so much as to please her guardian. She felt sharp disappointment when he returned her to Lady Grassmere and disappeared in the crowd.

Max fought back a yawn of boredom and glanced around the ballroom to see if he had done his duty by the dowagers and young girls. He caught sight of Amity, who was talking to Cousin Hester. His eyes kindled with warmth as the girl's mobile mouth broke into an impish grin. He wondered what mischief she was up to now. All in all, he was well pleased by her behavior this evening. Many a starchy tabby had whispered that she found Amity a very taking child. More to the point, Max had seen the gleam in several of the gentlemen's eyes as they took in the fresh beauty of the girl. He would soon have her off his hands, he mused, wondering why the thought gave him so little pleasure.

The evening was going well, and now he was free for the moment to pursue his own intentions. It took him little time to locate Honoria and less to cut her away from the men who surrounded her. Giving her his arm, he led her around the room until he was able to find a seat for her in a quiet window embrasure.

"Would you like something, my dear?" he asked solicitously as she carefully arranged her skirts on the red brocade cushion.

"Why, I have everything a young girl would require," Honoria said.

She bit off a coy giggle as she noticed his eyes wandering to his ward. His smile widened as the red-haired chit reached up to adjust the wreath of flowers on her head. Honoria's jaw tightened, and her eyes narrowed in thought until slowly her mouth turned up in a smile that had little to do with humor.

"Why, Max, you really must be congratulated," Honoria said.

"Congratulated?" Max said, turning to her in surprise.

"How ever did you convince your ward not to wear that awful dress?" She kept her eyes wide with innocence, although a shaft of pleasure shot through her at the guilty start from her companion. She lowered her voice just enough to indicate she was taking him into her confidence. "Your little ward is so impetuous. Argue though I might, I could

not convince her that she was making the wrong
choice."

"Wrong choice, my dear?" Max asked.

In a startled gesture Honoria raised her gloved
hand to her partially opened mouth. She dropped
her eyes as though overcome with shame that she
had spoken out of turn. She held the pose for a
second then raised her head, her eyes anguished
at the thought she had betrayed Amity. "Forgive
me, Max," she said in a whisper. "I thought you
knew."

"Knew what, Honoria?" He was thoroughly con-
fused. He had assumed that the ballgown had been
some sort of mistake, but now he wondered if he
should have questioned his ward further.

Honoria placed her hand on Max's sleeve and
sighed in resignation. "I would never have spoken
to you, but since Amity is your ward, I know you
will want to curb any tendencies she might have
that would make her unsuitable for the marriage
mart."

"I would appreciate anything you can tell me. I
have always known you had a fine eye for the proprieties and I must admit to a certain puzzlement.
What transpired at the dressmakers to have re-
sulted in the gown I saw earlier in the evening?"

"Was the gown dreadful?" Honoria asked as if
afraid to hear the answer.

"The gown did not suit the child," Max answered
stiffly.

"Oh la! I knew it would be thus. At least I was
afraid it might be," Honoria said in quick recovery.
"You see, my dear, our visits to Madame Bertoldi
did not go at all well."

"Why didn't you tell me?" Max asked in surprise. In the two weeks that Honoria and Amity had been going around town, there had not been the slightest hint that things were not as they should be. "Was the seamstress inadequate?"

Honoria caught her lower lip between her teeth and looked up at Max through a veil of lashes. "It must have been all my fault, Max," she said, her voice trembling slightly.

Max's heart was not impervious to the distress of the beautiful woman. He took her hand and raised it to his lips, and when he spoke his voice was caressing. "Come, my dear. You must know that I would never find fault with you. In my eyes you are perfection."

"Oh, you are too kind, Max, and I am a beast to treat you to such a display of emotion. It is that I did not know what to do, and I was so afraid that I would disappoint you." Honoria smiled wistfully, then retrieved her hand and placed it primly in her lap atop the other. "Amity is a delight, and it is laudable that she has rather, well, strong opinions. I tried to include her in the decisions when we were choosing her wardrobe. Her tastes are quite untutored, and I advised her where I could, but she would have only her way."

Honoria was pleased when Max began to scowl. She knew he was not angry with her, and she was very careful to choose her words so that she seemed to be defending Amity when in actual fact she was doing her best to undermine Max's confidence in the girl.

"The ball gown was her idea?"

"She said she had always dreamed of having

such a dress," Honoria said, sticking to the actual truth. The stupid girl had never an idea of how the gown would look on her tall figure. "I suggested several other styles, but she was not to be moved."

Max could understand now why Amity had looked so miserable. She was such an honest girl that she would have realized she had no one but herself to blame for such an error in judgment. He should have kept a closer eye on her instead of leaving poor Honoria to contend with her impetuousness. Tonight Miss Waterston looked rather tired, perhaps the result of dealing with his rambunctious ward. He would have to talk to Amity about being kinder to Honoria and more grateful for the advice the woman was so eager to give.

"No need to worry your pretty head, my dear. Now that Amity is launched, I can assume our trials are almost at an end."

Max stared across the ballroom and watched as his ward once again took the floor. It would seem that she had been a great success this evening. She was dancing with Lord Bancroft Paige, a rather priggish young man, but more than suitable. He was possessed of an ancient family name, unblemished with the slightest hint of scandal, and Max had it on good authority that the man was quite plump in the pocket. According to the latest *on dits*, Paige was hanging out for a wife.

"Bancroft looks quite taken with your ward," Honoria purred. "He would be an excellent prospect for the child."

"Perhaps," Max said slowly, his eyes intent on the flashing smile of his ward as she skipped through the pattern of the dance. "I'll admit he is good-looking, if she is partial to the Byronic ringlets of his blond hair. He may be a trifle young for Amity. He is only seven and twenty, after all. And, of course, his sister is a real tartar."

"Ophelia Paige?" she asked in feigned surprise. "Why, the child would be lucky to have such a steadying influence in her life. Ophelia would be more than happy to advise Amity."

Max snorted at the possibility of the dowdy woman giving Amity anything but harsh criticism. He had heard her speak disparagingly of the light-minded females who tried to ensnare her brother.

"You do intend to marry off the child?"

Honoria's abrupt question jolted Max from his reverie, and he spoke more sharply than usual, his words hearty to be more convincing. "Well naturally, my dear. That is the purpose of this evening after all. It is my dearest wish."

"And mine, also," Honoria said.

Her tone was low and the throaty quality surprised Max. When he glanced down at her, there was a definite invitation in her eyes, which he had not seen before. It was not that she was cold, but there was a certain aloofness about her that had always intrigued him. He felt guilty that he had not taken the time to mention his intentions to her, but no matter her willingness to accept his suit, this was not the proper time for a declaration.

"By the looks on the faces of several gentlemen here, I suspect there will be no absence of offers for my ward."

At his jocular tone an expression of dismay

touched Honoria's face; she had clearly expected to hear other words from his lips. Max patted her hand, but, noting the petulantly pursed lips, which would augur no good for the remainder of the evening, he quickly added, "Give me a smile, my dear. Once Amity is settled, I will have time and occasion to consider my own future."

Chapter Six

The late morning sun filtered through the sheer curtains of Amity's bedroom windows. She lay quietly, arms behind her head and smiled at the beautiful day. Contentment filled her as she remembered the magic of the ball the night before. Thanks to Max, the evening had been a total success; she was well launched in society.

For the first time since she had arrived in London, she felt like herself. She had been so caught up in the excitement of all the new experiences that she had lost sight of who she was. For the last several weeks she had been dominated by Honoria's personality and had tried to be someone she was not. She had resolved yesterday that she would take charge of her own life and see if she might make better use of her life. She had been living an artificial existence, letting others guide her and not being guided by what she knew was her own character and style. Perhaps her mistake had been in wanting so much to be approved of by both Max and Honoria that she allowed herself to be manipulated.

In her two weeks in London she had observed the

cynical, jaded manner of the elegant fashionable set and hated the thought of presenting such a picture of boredom. She felt a true excitement with life and did not want to lose that feeling. She suspected that Max was correct in that she must behave in a more ladylike manner, but she recognized that much of what her guardian criticized was basic to her character. She was impetuous by nature, prone to great bursts of enthusiasm and joy. It bothered her that in order to be acceptable, she would have to adopt a superficiality that went sorely against the grain. Much as she wanted to please Max, there must be some compromise she could work out to be both acceptable and herself.

Thus contented for the moment, Amity pushed herself up in the center of the bed and stretched her arms over her head in a satisfying stretch. She smiled at Muffin curled up at the foot of the bed. Every night when she went to sleep, the dog was nestled complacently on the rug by the fireplace, but when she woke in the morning, he was snoring peacefully on the comforter. Now ready to start the day, she prodded Muffin with her toes.

"What a lazybones you are," she said.

Muffin opened one eye and viewed her with disfavor, but Amity was impervious to censure. Tossing back the covers, she crawled to the foot of the bed, throwing her arms around the dog and hugging him enthusiastically. After a smothered snort of disdain, he favored her with a wet lick on the cheek, and as she scratched between his ears, he emitted a low growl of contentment.

" 'Bout time you're moving," Betta said, peeking around the opened door of the dressing room. "I was just about to come and see if you had taken up the ways of the fashionable set and were planning to sleep until afternoon."

"I should have known better than to hire an uppity servant," Amity said, grinning at the young girl. She bounded off the bed, sticking her nose in the air in great hauteur. Her pose was ruined somewhat when she bumped into a small table and stubbed her toe, but she tried to keep her face serious despite the giggles issuing from her abigail.

"Me mum would say that was the Good Lord's justice for being uncharitable to underlings."

"Besides, it is extremely uncomfortable," Amity said, ruefully wriggling the toes on her injured foot. "It's not easy being elegant, you know."

While Betta whisked around the room, Amity dressed, asking the girl how she liked her new position. She was enthusiastic over her reception by the other servants. Betta had been apprehensive that the replaced Pauline would be angry over her arrival, but after talking to the parlormaid was assured that she was welcome. Apparently Amity's assessment of Pauline's and the footman's interest in each other had been correct. Betta described the mooning looks the two servants had exchanged much to Amity's entertainment.

After dressing Amity hurried downstairs to breakfast, where Max was just finishing. Her guardian greeted her with congratulations for her successful debut.

"Lady Jersey has agreed to send you a voucher to Almack's," he announced, casting his eyes up to the ceiling and heaving a long sigh. "Now I shall be squiring you to the most boring of functions."

" 'Tis treasonous to speak such words," Amity said, shaking her head gravely at her guardian's pose. "I am enchanted to have received such an honor. Can't you tell by my serious demeanor?"

Max's eyes twinkled across the breakfast table. "It has occurred to me that you desire to cozen me by such behavior. Your eyes tell another story. Behind the sparkling color, mischief is apparent, just waiting to burst forth."

"La, sir, you malign me." Amity pouted, her face pulled into an expression of demure innocence.

"Baggage!"

On that happy note they exchanged smiles and began to talk of the evening past. Max informed her that bouquets of flowers and engraved invitations had arrived while she slept, proof positive of her acceptance. He asked her plans for the day and, when she told him she must visit Madame Bertoldi for final fittings on her wardrobe, offered the carriage. He debated telling her of his discussion with Honoria concerning the ballgown, but could not bear to criticize her in the face of her happiness. Time enough to discuss her stubborn refusal of Honoria's well-meant advice. As she blew him a kiss and scampered from the room, he returned to his coffee, surprised that he found little joy in the empty room now that the girl was gone. It was almost as if she had taken the sunshine with her when she left.

Collecting Betta and her bonnet and pelisse, Amity set off for the establishment of the modiste, Madame Bertoldi. When she arrived, she dismissed the carriage and entered the shop. She discovered the plump little woman lecturing a clerk over the placement of a particular bolt of fabric. Amity smiled at the darting hand gestures and flashing black eyes of the formidable Madame. When the woman became aware of her presence, a hint of wariness in the little Frenchwoman's eyes told Amity all that she needed to know about the wardrobe being prepared for her. The woman patted down her dress and tucked a graying strand of black hair into her disordered bun and crossed the floor. Amity felt sorry for the woman, who had been caught between Honoria and an unknown customer, and immediately set out to allay the seamstress's fears.

"Madame, a moment of your time." Amity pitched her voice softly so as not to be overheard by the curious assistants who hovered beyond the woman. "I have come to you to apologize for my foolishness."

The woman blinked rapidly several times, thrown off balance by the young lady's words. "A-apologize?" she stammered.

Leaning forward as though confessing a shameful secret, Amity continued, "I have been very stupid, Madame. In my excitement over choosing my own garments, I have not listened to the voice of experience in my dealings with you. It is only now that I realize I should have spoken to you earlier, but I am hoping that you will find it in your heart to forgive my youthful ignorance."

The sharp black eyes searched Amity's face, and her perception of the situation was immediate. "It is the wardrobe, *n'est pas?*"

"Yes, Madame. I fear that it will not do." She placed her hand on the agitated woman's arm, keeping her tone firm to command her attention.

"The bills I have incurred will be paid regardless. It is the realization that perhaps I might convince you to give me the benefit of your knowledge in striving for a more sophisticated look that has brought me to you today."

Once the practical Frenchwoman realized she would lose nothing financially, she capitulated entirely. In moments Amity was ensconced in her private sitting room with a cup of hot chocolate and a smiling Madame hovering over her. Assistants scurried about the room, laying out the nearly completed wardrobe on all the surfaces of the furniture. Looking at the dresses with a more objective eye, Amity had to admire the cleverness of Honoria. Each outfit was lovely in itself, but each one had one feature that made it unsuitable for Amity. In some cases the color of the dress washed out her own natural complexion, giving her a ghostly quality. In others the style of the dress was inappropriate, or the trim clashed with her red hair.

"What a waste," Amity muttered.

"C'est vrai," Madame responded over her shoulder.

Turning to the woman, Amity smiled. "My thought, Madame, is that with your help we can decide which of the outfits are totally unsuitable, and which others we can, shall we say, modify."

"Eh bien." The woman's voice was brisk with decision. "Please to sit down while I consider."

Amity subsided against the back of the cushioned chair and watched as the little woman bustled around the room. Her wrinkled face was pinched in concentration, and her mouth was pursed in a moue of distaste as she viewed each garment. Occasionally she glanced at Amity, her head cocked to the side and her eyes narrowed in study, then with a nod of her head she would return to an inspection of the offending article. Amity winked at Betta, who sat on the edge of her chair, and the girl relaxed, grinning in return.

To Madame's credit, once she had decided to involve herself she spared neither herself, her assistants, nor Amity. Each garment was tried on under the piercing eye of the modiste. Soon the room was littered with bolts of fabric, cards of trim, and other accessories. By unspoken agreement neither Madame nor Amity mentioned Honoria's name, although the deceitful blonde was on both of their minds. At the end of several hours, everything had been decided to everyone's satisfaction. The dresses that were deemed unsuitable had been given to the wide-eyed Betta to remake for herself, with others chosen to replace the missing items. The remainder would be altered, and, both Amity and Madame agreed, they would be the first stare of fashion.

"I feel very much relieved, Betta," Amity said as they exited the shop. "And it's a lovely day for a walk."

"Can't say as I'll mind," the practical abigail said as she sniffed the air. "That Madame uses a powerful lot of scent. Must be because she's a foreigner. Wouldn't like to work for her. She's a regular tartar the way she snaps out orders and stares down her nose at all those little assistants."

"You have to admit that she agreed to help without a single argument."

"She'd nothing to lose and everything to gain, if you ask me," Betta responded, unwilling to give an inch. "Didn't lose a cent, did she now, and you'll be wearing her clothes all over London and looking like a regular princess."

"Oh, I do like the sound of that," Amity chuckled. "I shall walk with my nose in the air, and everyone shall fall down in awe."

"More likely you'll do the falling, if you don't look where you're going."

Amity turned to grin at her abigail and a moment later crashed into a very substantial body. She whirled to apologize and was confronted by a handsome soldier whose empty sleeve was pinned to the shoulder of his uniform jacket. As she opened her mouth to speak, she noticed the sudden pallor of the man's face, and the dots of perspiration that had broken out on his forehead.

"Hartshorn, Betta," she whispered urgently, knowing her abigail always carried ample supplies of necessities.

While the girl dug in her reticule, Amity pushed the weakened man against the wall of the building, where he sagged, held up only by Amity's strong arms. Betta opened the vial and thrust it expertly beneath the soldier's nose. It took two whiffs before his eyes fluttered open, and his head jerked away from the burning aroma.

"Blimey," he said with disgust.

"Are you better?" Amity asked.

"I'll never smell again." His voice was raspy, but there was a rather shaky grin on his face, and his brown eyes twinkled at the two ladies now giggling at his words.

"I'm so sorry I bumped into you," Amity said.

"Did I hurt you badly?" She indicated his missing arm and his smile widened.

" 'Twas not me arm giving me trouble, miss, but me belly," he said. "I've neglected to eat much today, and I was feeling a bit rocky."

"Well that's easily attended to," Amity said taking charge of the situation in her usual high-handed manner. "Bring him along, Betta."

In his weakened condition the soldier was unable to gainsay the little abigail, and in no time at all, the three were seated in a nearby tearoom. Amity ordered sandwiches and pastries, and then introduced herself and Betta to the bemused young man.

"Jason Conway, miss. Was a sergeant before the Frogs took me arm. Been in London several days, and now I suspect I've died and gone to heaven, for I'm surely surrounded by angels."

Amity liked the look of the soldier with his curly thatch of hair and cheeky smile. Now that the color had returned to his face, he looked tan and healthy despite the missing arm. When the food arrived, he ate slowly and steadily, although she suspected his inclination was to cram everything into his mouth. It was apparent that it had been quite awhile since he had eaten, and his uniform was much the worse for wear. If not penniless, he was close to it.

"What did you do before the war, Jason?" Amity asked as she sipped her tea.

"Worked for a solicitor. I've a head for numbers, though lot of use that'll do me," he said, bitterness creeping into his voice for the first time.

"Why ever not?"

"There's many a soldier back from the war that finds that there are no jobs available. Can't work without a recommendation, and the army's not much of a reference."

"I see," Amity said, exchanging glances with Betta, who remembered clearly being in a similar situation. "Are there many men out of work?"

"Plenty, miss, and it's a bleeding shame. Begging your pardon, ladies," he said nodding to Amity and Betta. "There's more coming to London every day, and the government has done nothing to provide for ex-soldiers."

"Surely someone should do something," Amity said, placing her cup in the saucer with a decisive clink of china.

"A few of us have gotten together to pool our resources. Those that got jobs try and help those what ain't."

"Have you tried the agencies?" Betta interjected.

"No good, miss. Not without a character."

"There must be hundreds of jobs in this city," Amity said. "All we'd need to do is locate a few, and then as word got out, we could find others. I've made a lot of friends since I arrived, and I could ask if they have need of any staff."

Jason glanced at Betta as if to ask if her mistress were slightly deranged, and the abigail patted his arm for encouragement.

"It's just Miss Amity's way," she said quietly. "She does tend to leap into things, but she's of good heart. I know it's presumptuous of us to intrude on your affairs, but in this case, I think she might have an idea."

While Betta and Jason had been talking, Amity's mind was busy. She had been feeling quite useless since her arrival in town. Used to managing the affairs of Beech House, she could not spend all of her time attending parties and shopping. She liked the idea that she could somehow put her talents for getting to know people to some advantage. Her thoughts jumped from one problem to another. Suddenly she looked at Betta and Jason, a wide smile spreading across her face.

"I have just thought of an excellent idea. My guardian has a large staff both in the town house and the stables. I can talk to Putnam and see if we might not take on a few extra men. They could work for several weeks, and then I will write them a recommendation. The letter need not specify how long they worked for Lord Kampford. Do you think that might work?"

Jason opened his mouth, but no words came out. He could not quite believe that she was serious, and yet when he glanced at the abigail, the girl nodded her head in agreement.

"I do believe you are an angel," he finally growled, his voice unnaturally hoarse. "Would you really do that?"

"Well of course I will, Jason. After all, you fought for my freedom too, so it's only fair that I do something for you. I shall speak to Putnam this afternoon, and you shall send round several men. Now then," she continued briskly, "what shall we do with you?"

"Me, miss?" Jason asked. "I thought I might be one of the servants."

"Piffle. A man good with numbers is hard to find. Let me see." She stared at the table, her face pinched in concentration. "Bircher? No. Ah! Burgess. Mr. Johannas Burgess. He's the man for you."

"If I might inquire, miss," Jason said, grinning across at the efficient Miss Fraser, "just who is Johannas Burgess?"

"Man's an importer I've corresponded with for several years. My estate manager, Henderson, put me onto him, and I've found him quite useful in the past. In fact, if I'm not mistaken"—Amity stared out the windows at the busy street beyond—"we're not far from his office."

Once more Jason Conway found himself in the clutches of Betta, while Amity paid the charges and started out the door. He and the little abigail had to hurry to keep up with the rapid footsteps of the bustling Miss Fraser and were breathless by the time they arrived at their destination.

"I'll just duck in here and have a word with Mr. Burgess. Please to wait, Jason. We shall be out presently."

Thus saying, she left the astonished man and disappeared up the stairs of the building, followed by her abigail. Jason never knew what was said, but when she returned, he had a position starting the next day and a week's advance on his salary for suitable clothing and food. Before he could do more than babble his thanks, she was taking her leave.

"I shall send Betta around with a message, if I am successful with Putnam, but I have little doubt, he will be happy to cooperate," she said blithely. "We shall meet soon and work out a more thorough plan. Good day, Mr. Conway."

Amity and Betta discussed the problem all the way back to the town house. The abigail suggested that she might ask among the servants in other houses and thus widen their circle of opportunity.

The servants' network was highly efficient. There was little that went on upstairs that the downstairs brigade was not aware of. Amity was delighted with the whole project and immediately went to work cajoling Putnam into hiring a few of the soldiers. Their project was now off to a good start.

A week later her wardrobe began to arrive, and Amity was anxious to show off her new garments. Standing in front of the mirror, she felt truly elegant. The lime green walking dress was tailored to show off her slim figure. The darker green trim on the edge of the jacket minimized her height and was repeated at the wrists and again at the bottom of her skirt. Now that she was correctly dressed, she was eager to be abroad and suitably accompanied by Betta, and the ever present Muffin, made her way out of the town house for a walk in the park. It was several hours later that she glanced in dismay at her lapel watch.

"Oh, Betta, we're late for luncheon again," Amity said, hurrying through the gates of the park. "Lady Grassmere made me promise just two days ago that I would be more careful of the time."

Amity sighed heavily, aware of her shortcomings, but there were so many sights to see in London that every time she went out she forgot to pay much attention to the passage of time.

"Miss Amity," Betta called breathlessly, trying to keep pace with the longer strides of her mistress. Even Muffin had fallen behind, and the abigail called once again. "Miss Amity, have mercy. I can't keep up with your steps, and if his lordship sees you, he will not think you are behaving in a proper ladylike manner."

"Blast!"

"Miss Amity!" Betta cried in horror. "You promised his lordship you wouldn't say that dreadful word."

Amity stopped so suddenly in her tracks that the hurrying little figure promptly bumped into her back. The sight of the heaving bosom of her breathless abigail immediately brought an expression of contrition to Amity's frowning countenance. She heaved a sigh of resignation.

"It is prodigiously difficult to be a lady," Amity muttered. "Every rule seems to contradict another. Don't be late! Don't rush! Now really, Betta, I cannot do both."

The little abigail grinned cheekily at her mistress. "It's a sorry life you lead."

"Hah! Great lot of sympathy you give me." Amity returned the grin, then tapped her foot impatiently as she stared at Muffin, who was slowly padding his way to join them. "Come along, old fellow. If you cannot hold a better pace than that, we shall leave you behind."

The dog raised reproachful eyes to his mistress's face, but did not in any way indicate that he was bothered by the threat. He was almost abreast of the two girls when the sound of loud cursing forced him to stop once more.

"Move, you bleedin' bag of bones!"

A whip cracked, and Amity's attention was caught by the sight of a dilapidated cart drawn by a nag of ancient, though not necessarily noble, lineage. The carter was standing up in his seat, in turn berating and whipping the pathetic horse. A feeling of rage filled Amity and without hesitation she stalked to the side of the cart.

"Blast ye! Git along!" shouted the carter, laying about with his whip.

"Stop that caterwauling at once, you ruffian!" Amity demanded.

The very unexpectedness of the sight of the fashionably dressed young lady caused the carter to lose his balance, and as his arms flailed to keep from falling off his perch, he dropped the whip. Amity pounced on the offending article, snatching it off the cobblestones and glaring up at the choleric face of the man.

"For shame, you blackguard," Amity sneered, her voice an icy stream of contempt. "To treat this fine animal so cruelly."

The mare in question drooped in her traces, unaware of the tumult raging over her head. Betta moved closer to her mistress, as if her slight figure might protect the raging amazon who had so forgotten herself as to create a public disturbance.

"Miss Amity," Betta hissed in agony. "Do come away. What will his lordship say?"

"Stop your fussing, girl. Would you have me abandon a creature in need of protection?"

Amity waved her hand in the general direction of the pathetic animal in front of the cart. There was a bedraggled pink ribbon tied around her forelock, which hung in tattered elegance over one eye. The malnourished mare was brown in color with a coat in dire need of grooming. There were patches of white around her neck where the rubbing harness had worn away the hair, and spots of noisome splatters on her legs and chest. Her tail and mane were tangled and greasy, as dirty as the rest of the beast. But to Amity it made little difference if the horse were not a thoroughbred. She could not abide turning away from such a disgraceful sight.

"G'way with you!" the red-faced man bellowed, staring belligerently at the red-haired miss. " 'Tis no affair of yourn."

"It most certainly is," Amity said, drawing herself up with great dignity. "It is every citizen's concern to right the wrongs of injustice. England is not a country where one can pass by while a poor dumb beast is whipped. And a female at that. For shame."

"Bloody 'ell!" The carter threw down his reins and clambered out of the cart to stand towering over the impassioned young lady. "And gi'e me my whip, you interfering little . . ."

"Silence, you knave! Would you add blasphemy to your already long list of offenses?" Although Amity felt some slight danger from the outraged man, the press of a cold nose against her skirts alerted her to the presence of reinforcements, and her courage was immediately bolstered. "Belay that noise, or I shall set my dog upon you."

Unfortunately Muffin, exhausted from his brisk walk, chose that particular moment to lie down. The carter guffawed loudly, snatching his cap off to slap it enthusiastically against his leg. This action caused a cloud of noxious odor to escape from his filthy clothing, and Amity stepped back in disgust.

"Gawd love ya, miss," the man roared in amusement. His mouth lolled open presenting a wide, gap-toothed grin. "You must be a bleedin' bedlamite."

Amity recovered and glared furiously up at the man. She raised the whip, poking the tip against the man's chest to emphasize her words. "Have you no conscience, man? The animal is blown. Beating her will gain you nothing but a dead horse."

"Gi'e over, miss." The cowardly man flinched away from the point of the whip. "The 'orse is mine to deal with."

"You shall not beat her again, sirrah!"

Amity could feel Betta pulling on the sleeve of her pelisse, but her compassion for the poor animal forced her to ignore her abigail. The loathsome carter glared at her and leaned forward until his face was close to her own. When he spoke, the stench of his breath made her eyes water.

"If I choose to beat 'er, I will. The 'orse is mine."

"I will not permit you to touch her," she said icily.

"The 'orse is mine!"

"Then I'll buy the bloody horse!" Amity shouted, exasperated beyond all measure.

The sound of applause greeted this salvo, and Amity spun around in dismay. Her face flushed in horror as she realized the scene had drawn a crowd of spectators. Although she was mortified, she refused to back down and decided the sooner she finished the business, the quicker she could get away. Reaching for her reticule, she tore open the strings and delved inside for some coins.

"How m-much?" she stammered, all too aware of the interested crowd pressing around her.

Seeing the embarrassment on the young girl's face, the crafty owner knew that revenge was close at hand. His face split in a toothy grin, and very slowly, enjoying her discomfort, he extended his grimy hand. "Two pounds," he announced with triumph.

"Well of all the gall," she snapped in returning anger. "You cannot be serious, man."

"Your very words were that the 'orse were a fine animal. She's worth every penny of the price."

"You must have been a highwayman in your younger days, you wretch," Amity muttered. She edged closer, dropping her voice to a coaxing tone. "Look here, good fellow, let's have an end to this haggling. These are all the coins I have with me." Hiding her hand from the ring of spectators, she opened it carefully to give the man a glimpse of the contents. "If you say me nay, I shall leave, and you will have on your hands only a half-dead horse. If you agree, I'll put the coins in my reticule and hand you the purse. You can brag to everyone that you drove a hard bargain, and I shall not gainsay you."

Amity had guessed to a nicety that the man was eager to save face before the crowd. Greed was apparent in his squinty eyes, and he licked his lips once before nodding his head with a jerky movement. On cue Amity jammed the coins inside the purse and, shaking her head in chagrin, handed it to the triumphantly grinning carter. The crowd cheered, and her face flushed at once more being the center of their attention.

"Lord love ya, Miss Amity," Betta cried, her face ashen with worry. "How ever are you going to explain this to his lordship?"

Amity gulped at the mention of her guardian, but bravely shrugged away her concern. "I shall tell him the horse followed me home."

She watched the carter free the horse from her

traces and then loop a dirty rope through the halter. She stepped forward and extended her gloved hand to accept the lead rope.

" 'Er name's Guinevere," the man said, guffawing loudly.

"I would have guessed as much."

Amity turned to lead the horse away, and the crowd cheered once more, shouting words of encouragement, which made her blush. Raising her chin, she started down the street calling to Betta and Muffin as she went. She had only gone a short way when she heard a squeal from her abigail and turned to the girl, who was frozen in her tracks, a look of horror suffusing her face.

"Lawks, miss!" Betta hissed. "It's his lordship."

"It needed only that," Amity muttered glumly.

She groaned, wondering if it were possible to disappear off the face of the earth. There was nothing for it then but to brazen it out. Cautiously she turned her head just as her guardian's carriage drew abreast of her. The window was down and Max, his green eyes flashing under narrowed lids, was framed in the opening.

"And where are you off to with your merry little band?" Max drawled.

Amity gritted her teeth at his bantering tone and raised her chin with great dignity. Perhaps the impression she hoped to give was slightly diminished when the mare stumbled, but she kept her eyes firmly fixed to a spot above her guardian's head and pretended she had noticed nothing amiss. "I am for home," she said.

"Can I assume you are accompanied by a new addition to our happy household?"

"Yes, milord. I have just purchased the mare."

"Plans for a stud farm?" he asked.

"She needed a home," Amity said quietly.

"So it would seem." Max, his face a bland mask, stared at the horse, the abigail, and the mangy dog. "Mayhap in your busy schedule, you might find time to have a brief chat with me in the library? I shall, of course, await your pleasure," Max said, his tone a stream of ice. "In the meantime perhaps I might be of some service. Lewis?"

The footman leaped to the ground and hurried to the open window of the carriage. "Aye, milord."

"I realize it is much to ask, but if you will be so kind as to relieve Miss Fraser of her enchanting prize, I would be most appreciative."

"With pleasure, milord," Lewis said, trying to keep his mouth from twitching into a grin.

"Take, eh . . ." Max paused delicately, cocking an inquiring eyebrow at Amity.

"Guinevere," Amity snapped, tired of the game.

"A noble name indeed," Max intoned. "Take the Lady Guinevere around to the mews and ask Dobson to do what he can. Now, unless there is something more that I can do, I shall be off. Good day, Miss Fraser."

Max raised the carriage window and tapped on the roof with his walking cane. He had one more glimpse of the odd little tableau before the carriage jerked away from the scene. It was just as well, since it was only a moment before he could no longer stem the rolling laughter that welled up in his chest. He laughed until his eyes were streaming as he remembered more and more details of Amity's disgraceful conduct.

Chapter Seven

Amity sat on a bench in the sun. A book was spread open on her lap, pillowed on the sprigged-muslin skirts. A straw bonnet was perched on her red curls and the ever present Muffin was sprawled at her feet. Beside her was the neatly dressed abigail, her hands busy sorting a lap full of wildflowers.

"It's been a busy week, Betta," Amity said. "You've done a wonderful job, you know."

"It was really just a matter of talking to people," Betta said. Her face was flushed with pleasure at her mistress's words. "You know how I love to chatter."

"How many do you think the runners will take?"

"Aimsley said he would consider taking on four men. I was hoping for more, but he said as how he would have to see how this batch worked out." Betta picked up one of the flowers she had gathered, her fingers stroking the petals as she talked. "It was a brilliant idea to think of the Bow Street Runners, Miss Amity."

"Well, it seemed fairly logical since it's so much like the army." She sighed, turning a page of the book in her lap. She frowned down at the print, not really seeing the letters. "There are so many men out of work, Betta, and it seems like it is going so slowly."

"Lawks, miss, we've already placed twenty men and that's not even counting the four today. And," she said, her voice quivering with excitement, "I've made friends with a woman who works for the Duke of Clarence."

"You never!" Amity said, clapping her hands in excitement. "Holding out on me, you wretched girl!"

Betta giggled and hid her laughter behind a quickly raised hand. "It just happened this morning, and I haven't had a moment to tell you. I was at the market, and we got to jabbering. Just friendly like. When she told me where she worked you could have blown me over with a feather. I asked if she could get away for tea someday, and she agreed."

"Just imagine," Amity cooed. "The duke must have an enormous staff. There should be plenty of places available."

"Here comes Mr. Conway." Betta's voice was an excited whisper, and Amity noted the becoming blush of color that dotted each cheek.

Jason Conway looked far different from the threadbare soldier they had first met. He was dressed neatly in a black suit with a plain white shirt and well-polished shoes. He strode with a jaunty air; the cloth cap covering his curly brown hair was cocked over his sparkling brown eyes. Approaching the bench, he snatched off his cap before bowing to the ladies.

"Good day to ye, Miss Fraser, and to you also, Miss Betta."

Amity was amused that Jason gave her only a cursory glance before his eyes shifted for a more thorough perusal of her abigail. Betta played with the flowers in her lap, her flaming cheeks the only sign of her awareness of the young man. Muffin raised his head, giving a low, whining sound, and the young man dropped to one knee to greet the dog.

"Allo, old beastie," he crooned, scratching between Muffin's ears. "Feels good, don't it, old boy?"

"You're sounding extremely chipper, Jason," Amity said. "All is well with you?"

The young man scrambled to his feet, brushing the dog hairs from his jacket. "Oh, aye, Miss Fraser. Mr. Burgess has been very good to me, and I'm that happy in my work." Although he spoke to Amity, she had the feeling that he was directing every word to her companion. "The importer's office is large, and there's much room for advancement. After only a few weeks he has taken a shine to me. Says I have a good head for figures, miss, if you'll pardon me boasting."

"You'll go far, Jason. I have great faith in you. Now, here is the latest set of recommendations and some money for clothing," she said, handing him a bulky envelope, which he kissed with a great show of reverence before slipping it inside his jacket. "Make sure the men are properly scrubbed and wearing something suitable before they go to see Aimsley. He's willing to take four men on as runners."

"Cooee! You are a proper wonder!" Jason said, his mouth flashing in a wide grin of pleasure.

"Far from it, I fear. Actually your accolades are misplaced since Betta was responsible for convincing Aimsley to hire on the men."

Jason turned to the abigail. His face held an expression of wonderment as he stared at the modestly bent head. He coughed and Betta raised her face, staring back at him with eyes alight with pleasure. "I a d my friends are most grateful for your help, Miss Betta."

" 'Twere nothing, Mr. Conway. I am conscious of how it feels to be in desperate straits," she said softly.

"To think you went to Aimsley yourself. You're a brave one, Miss Betta."

Amity sighed at the romantic pair. She could tell that a genuine liking had sprung up between them in just the short time they had been working together. She hoped for Betta's sake that Jason would prove to be a steadfast suitor for the girl's affection. She let the twosome chatter for several minutes, but after glancing at her lapel watch, Amity coughed to bring them back to the business at hand.

"I have arranged to have one of our footmen collect used clothing at some of the larger houses each week. The ladies of my acquaintance are quite pleased to feel they are doing their part for a worthwhile cause."

"There's plenty of men that will be pleased to have the clothes. They're not all that particular about who wore them last. Here's a list of the men that'll be coming to work for Mr. Putnam come Fri-

day. I've vetted them all and they're good, trust-
worthy lads."

"The last batch worked out quite splendidly.
Dobson suggested young Henry stay on, but the boy
wants to work somewhere in the country," Amity
said. "Well I guess that's all for this week. We'll
see you next Tuesday."

"Righto, Miss Fraser. I'm off, then," Jason said,
bowing once more. As he turned, he winked broadly
at Betta, touching his cap with two fingers in a
lighthearted salute.

"Your young man is a charmer, my girl," Amity
said, smiling at her abigail, whose eyes were following the rapidly disappearing figure.

"Go on with you, Miss Amity. He's never my
young man," Betta said, but she returned her mistress's grin with one of her own. "Not that he
couldn't be, if I said the word."

The girls laughed companionably, then gathered
Muffin and their belongings and started back along
the path, well contented with their afternoon adventure.

Sitting in a leather chair in the library, Max was
immersed in a book and heard the low voices and
the sound of scurrying feet with only a portion of
his mind. A shrill squeal, the tinkle of broken
crockery, and quickly smothered curses alerted him
to the possibility that all was not running as usual
in his household. He closed the book, placing a finger inside to save his place. Then heaving an exasperated sigh, he pushed himself out of the chair
and strode to the door. His footsteps were silent on
the floor runner, and he arrived at the corner of the

balcony overlooking the entrance hall without giving away his presence. Still clutching the book, he rested his arms on the railing, keeping well in the shadow of the wall, and leaned forward so that he might better take in the astounding scene below.

Putnam, the starchy, white-haired butler, stood with his back to the front door, arms outstretched as if to prevent a legion from attacking his stronghold. Two liveried footmen, hunched over for the best effect, were stalking a small animal across the black and white marble of the foyer. A parlor maid, no doubt the author of the high-pitched scream, stood in the entrance to the kitchen hallway, her apron pressed in a wad over her mouth. As if that was not enough activity, Mrs. Putnam was sweeping up the remnants of a small vase, which used to stand on the hall table.

Since this was not the normal conduct of his servants in his well-ordered household, Max was decidedly curious. The most amazing part of the scene was that instead of loud shouting the entire procedure was being conducted in whispers.

"Move to your right, Lewis," Putnam ordered. "Right, I said, you dunderhead."

"I do not like the look in its eye, Mr. Putnam," Lewis whispered back.

"Stop it, you imbecile." The harassed butler wiped his forehead on the impeccable sleeve of his jacket. "It's not a wild boar, you know. It's only a bloody babe."

Now that the footman had moved, Max was able to see that it was indeed a small, black and white piglet. Max cocked his head in puzzlement. He did not know much about the details of running his establishment, but he did not think that the kitchen staff was purchasing live animals for the consumption of the household. Curiously he watched.

The larger of the two footman circled to the left and made a brave lunge for the pig, but slipped on the marble floor, sprawling across the foyer. Lewis, aided by his youth and speed, hurled himself in the path of the piglet, whose hooves scrabbled ineffectually, unable to find purchase on the slick surface. In a flurry of arms and legs, the young footman was able to capture the loudly squealing animal against his chest.

Putnam abandoned his post at the door, clapping the young man on the shoulder as he scrambled off the floor. "Well done, lad," he congratulated the boy in a low voice. "Now get that beast back out to the storeroom and be more careful in the future."

"Sorry, Mr. Putnam." The boy's face was flushed with pleasure at the butler's praise. "I know I shouldn't 'ave brought it into the 'ouse. Some of them in the kitchen 'adn't seen any of the little fellows, and I was just showing this one off. I set 'im down on the floor, and the bloody thing bolted right between me legs."

"No harm done," Putnam said, his face disapproving as he eyed the broken vase on the floor. "Praise God, it was not a family heirloom. All right then, get back to your duties. In future, Pauline, we shall have no more caterwauling."

"It's sorry, I am, Mr. Putnam," the parlormaid said, wringing her apron. "I thought it was an enormous rat."

"What on earth would a rat be doing in his lordship's house?" The butler sounded decidedly aghast

at the mere suggestion, and without another word
the shamefaced maid vanished down the hallway
toward the kitchen. "A rat indeed!" Putnam
snorted as he turned to his wife.

Mrs. Putnam was placing the last of the shards
of pottery in the cradle of her apron. She gave the
floor one last swipe with the broom and then spoke
to Putnam, while her eyes circled the foyer to es-
tablish the fact that all was returned to normal.

"You better put a bee in Miss Amity's ear, love,"
she said, folding the apron over the remains of the
vase and clutching it to her ample bosom. She
hoisted the broom to her shoulder in military precision, where it rested looking slightly incongruous
against the lace cap that topped her steel gray hair.

"I'll speak to her the very moment she comes in,
cupcake."

Putnam's tone was a combination of a wheedle
and a leer, which, coupled with the unexpected en-
dearment, almost sent the voyeur on the balcony
into convulsions. Max eased himself back into the
shadow of the wall, unwilling to be caught eaves-
dropping, yet reluctant to miss the end of the scene.

"She'll have to send one of her soldiers," the
woman continued. "The garden storeroom is getting a dash crowded since the old sow had twelve
in the litter. Besides which, the goat has eaten the
stuffing out of one of the chairs that was stored
there."

"Never mind, mother," Putnam said, patting his
wife on her well-padded bottom. "I'll take care of
it."

"See that you do," Mrs. Putnam said with a sniff

that turned into a giggle as she hurried across the foyer.

Max slipped around the corner and, walking quietly, returned to the comforting silence of the library. He dropped into the leather chair and placed the forgotten book on the ornate Chinese table at his elbow. Occasionally a chuckle of amusement escaped him as he replayed the scene in his mind. He wondered if he would ever be able to look Mrs. Putnam in the eye without thinking of her as "cupcake" and disgracing himself thoroughly by laughing.

Although the entire episode had been most entertaining, he was aware that he was far from enlightened over the meaning of it all. There was obviously something havey-cavey going on in his household, and the intriguing Miss Amity Fraser seemed to be at the very center of the conspiracy. He rested his head against the cool leather headrest, his face screwed into a frown of concentration.

Questions whirled in his mind. What was a piglet doing in the front hall? And had a sow actually littered in the garden storeroom? Surely Mrs. Putnam hadn't really mentioned a goat? What did she mean by the reference to Amity's soldier? And why in tarnation did the whole group of servants seem to be involved in something bizarre and yet treat it as an everyday occurrence?

"Blast the girl!" Max muttered. "What form of mischief is she up to now?"

He remembered clearly that Amity had asked his permission to use the storeroom that attached to the garden shed, but for the life of him he could not recall her mentioning any specific purpose. She had also asked for an increase in her allowance, and he wondered if she were purchasing the livestock. But for what purpose?

In the two months since he had first taken on the personal responsibility for his ward, the chit had put paid to his quiet bachelor existence. His well-run household was a shambles, and his personal affairs were constantly being disrupted. He had assumed when he invited her to London, he would be little aware of her presence in the spacious town house. After all, the girl had a chaperon and a full schedule of activities. Other than an occasional dinner together and squiring her to various social functions, he should be reasonably free of her presence or even a reminder of her existence.

He glowered across the room at an untidy pile of books on the window seat. There were flowers on the table in the center of the room, the yellow daisies a great splash of color against the warm wood tones in the rest of the room. On the carpet beside the green velvet wing chair near the fireplace was a basket of sewing, and on the small table there was a crumpled pair of mittens marking the place in an opened book. The girl had made serious inroads on his private sanctum.

In actual fact, Max was constantly being reminded of the girl's presence. There was not a room in the house that did not show some sign of change, with the sole exception of his bedroom. Here his eyes narrowed, and he sighed in defeat as he remembered the flowers on his bedside table. Wilberforce, his valet, had announced that Miss Amity had given him the filled vase with strict instructions as to its placement. Although the little man had worn a disapproving frown at such a feminine conceit, Max noticed that the vase was never empty. Fading blooms changed with Wilberforce's usual degree of efficiency.

Looking at the clock, Max was reminded of his engagement to take Honoria for a drive. He did not have the time to march out to the garden and find out for himself just exactly what was going on. On second thought, he admitted, he was procrastinating because he did not want to know. Resolving to eventually get to the bottom of the puzzling scene he had witnessed, he hurried along to his bedroom. His valet awaited him, his wizened face set in disapproval at the unseemly haste of his master. Wilberforce believed that the art of dressing should be conducted in an atmosphere of dignified leisure. The little man still regretted Max's conversion to a more sober style. The dandy stage had really kept the servant on his mettle.

Too tired to argue with his valet, Max put himself in Wilberforce's efficient hands and was soon dressed more formally than he would have wished. Outside, his carriage was waiting, and as he climbed in, the coachman gave the horses the signal to start.

Still feeling grossly put upon by the machinations of his ward, Max glared out the window at the passing scene. Amity was wreaking havoc on the smooth running of his household. There was something peculiar going on. Was it conceivable that he was harboring a sow, twelve piglets, and a goat beneath his very roof?

"Devil take it!" he swore. "What next?"

When he had decided to sponsor the chit, he had

never envisioned that it would in any way interfere
with his normal way of life. He liked his bachelor
comforts and the predictable events that took place
in his household. He would have an end to it, he
decided. It was time to rid his household of the disturbing presence of Miss Amity Fraser; time for him
to stop shilly-shallying and locate a respectable
suitor for the girl. He would marry her off immediately, and then he could get back to his peaceful
existence.

After ten minutes spent with Honoria, Max was
reminded of what a thoroughly restful woman she
was. She was everything a lady should be, a combination that Max found soothing to his lacerated
emotions. She was composed, aloof, and did not
chatter away, making him privy to all her thoughts
and feelings. She was not forever fluttering around,
smiling and joking as if life was a great joy. In fact,
since he had known Honoria, she had never given
him a moment of worry. Just looking at the lovely
creature was balm to the soul.

Honoria's gown was the last word in fashion.
Yards and yards of shimmering yellow silk bil-
lowed across the seat, giving the illusion of some
golden flowerlike creature. One gloved hand held a
white lace fan, and the other rested atop the jew-
eled handle of a dainty parasol of matching yellow
silk. Her blond hair was smoothed into a bun at the
base of her neck and a shower of ribbons fluttered
from the stiff brim of a saucy straw hat.

Max frowned at a sudden remembrance of the
wild curls of his ward. He had finally convinced her
to dress it properly, and it was now generally re-
strained in a net or bound up in a coronet of braids.

He had noticed, however, that despite her efforts at control, an occasional curl escaped the confinement and dangled temptingly against her white cheek.

"How cross you look, Max," Honoria said, interrupting his thoughts. "Have I done something to displease you?"

"My apologies, my dear. I was in a brown study when I arrived, but the pleasure of your company has done much to lighten my mood."

"You have seemed preoccupied of late," she said. "I hope taking your delightful ward to all the social affairs has not been too great a burden for you. I know men prefer other pursuits over a round of routs and balls."

"How understanding you are." Max reached across to pat her hand. He wished he were sitting beside her, but she hadn't liked having her skirts crushed so he was sitting with his back to the horses. "It has been a dash wearying, but I believe my duties are nearly at an end."

"Have you finally received an offer for the girl?"

"I have received several offers already," Max answered stiffly, unwilling to let Honoria think the girl was a complete antidote. Then waving his hand as if it was of no consequence, he continued, "I turned them all down."

"Turned them down?" Honoria's voice was shrill in surprise. To cover her lapse she breathed deeply, fixing an expression of curiosity on her face. "Were they not good offers?"

"Well, yes. And then again, no." Max shifted uncomfortably on the seat. "Dodsworth is a second son, and he had his eye on her dowry. I suspect he liked her well enough, but I did not think they would suit."

"I see," Honoria said.

"Lord Haines is run up on tick. He would gamble everything away in a sennight. And of course, General Cuthburton is sixty if he's a day." Max snorted in disgust.

"Perhaps the child would deal well with a man of his age," she purred. "He wears his years exceedingly well. Very distinguished. The child could do much worse."

"I'll not have it," Max snapped, staring out bleakly at the passing scene. The thought of that desiccated old man touching Amity was physically repugnant to him.

"Is that all?" Honoria asked. She closed her fan with a snap, her fingers crushing the lacy accessory.

"Well, Fairchild was expected, and even Winfield put in a bid, but I did not see them as serious offers."

"Is there anyone who hasn't offered for the girl?" Honoria found it difficult to keep the acid out of her voice.

"Bancroft Paige. Can't imagine what is taking the man so long. But I assume eventually he will come up to scratch," Max said wearily. "In fact, he has asked for an appointment tomorrow at ten."

"How wonderful," Honoria said. She reached across and tapped Max gently on the wrist with her fan. "Surely, my dear, you can have nothing against the man."

"He has been underfoot now for the last few weeks. Amity seems to enjoy his company, and his manners are unexceptionable." Max stroked his jawline as he tried to analyze why he was not more delighted with the young man.

"He is a truly eligible parti, Max. And so very handsome. Why, any girl would be thrilled to have fixed his interest."

"I don't know if Amity is particularly thrilled, but at least she does not dismiss the man as she has so many others. Says they have no serious thoughts in their heads. Can you imagine?" Max seemed genuinely nonplussed by her attitude. "Not that I think Paige has any great depth."

"She is very young, Max," Honoria said, her voice patronizing. "She needs a steadying influence. Bancroft Paige is serious enough despite his handsome looks."

Max nodded his head in agreement, wondering why Honoria kept repeating how handsome the man was. Certainly he was good-looking, but after all, a head of blond curls was not the end-all. However, the more he thought of it, the more convinced he became that Paige might be an eligible suitor for Amity. He had little humor and was a bit puffed up with his own consequence, but there was clearly nothing particularly wrong with the man. Then a thought occurred to Max, and he leaned toward Honoria.

"What of his sister?" he asked. "Rather prune-faced woman. A thirty-year-old spinster might not make the best companion for a young wife."

Honoria's light tinkling laughter echoed inside the carriage, and Max relaxed at the charming sound. "Ophelia is really a darling," she said. "She is shy in company, so she hides behind that brusque manner. She will be a good friend to Amity."

The furrows in Max's forehead smoothed out and he leaned back against the squabs. He felt convinced that his problems were over. His household would be peaceful again. Soon he could be about settling his own future. He smiled across at the golden vision, content that his planning would soon come to fruition.

Chapter Eight

Lord Bancroft Paige was perched on the edge of a chair in front of the mahogany desk, his polished boots primly together, and his hands on the knees of his elegantly tailored biscuit-colored trousers. Although Max had made small talk in order to put the man at his ease, all his best efforts had been wasted. Like a primed pump, Paige was ready to blurt out his news at the least opening.

"Saw you at Tattersall's last week," Max said, leaning back in the leather chair and stretching his legs. "Were you after the bays or that black stallion?"

"The bays, sir," Bancroft said. For the first time in the interview he relaxed against the back of the chair. "A pair of sweet goers if I ever saw them. Thought to add them to my stable, but Percy Waterston was before me. Quite frankly I was surprised since I thought the man was sadly dipped."

"I had heard some such story, but I hadn't given it much thought," Max drawled. In actual fact, he had given it a great deal of thought. Since he planned to offer for Honoria, it concerned him that rumors persisted that her brother was an inveterate gambler. The times that he had seen Percy, he found the stories only too credible. And now to purchase those bays. Must have had a run of luck. "Did you find any other cattle to suit?"

" 'Fraid not, sir," Bancroft said, his expression glum. "Thought the bays would have shown well. I must admit, I was hoping to impress your ward."

"Amity? I fear you're well out there. Miss Fraser is rarely impressed with the normal run-of-the-mill thoroughbred," he smiled in remembrance. "You must ask her sometime to show you Lady Guinevere, a mare she purchased only recently."

"A hunter?" Bancroft asked.

"I shouldn't think so," Max said, shaking his head. "Although at this point it's most difficult to tell."

"Beg pardon, sir?"

"Devil take it, Paige," Max snapped in exasperation, bringing the man to sharp attention on his chair. "If you call me sir one more time, I shall throw you out on the street. Makes me feel positively decrepit. By gad, sir, I can't be above five years older than you. Call me Max."

"My apologies, si—Max," Bancroft stammered, all too conscious of the dangerous gleam in the man's eye. "I was trying to show proper respect."

"Get on with it, Bancroft. I seem to be in an ill humor today, but it has little to do with your errand." Max rubbed the back of his neck, wondering why he was feeling so savage. He knew why Paige had requested the interview, and he should be delighted. He sighed in resignation, determined to be gracious. "Was there anything special you wished to see me about?"

"Well, yes." Bancroft edged to the front of the chair, fussily smoothing the material over one knee before he raised his head. His face was flushed, and in the early morning light, a sheen of perspiration glimmered on his forehead. "It is about your ward."

"Miss Fraser? How singular." Now that the time had come, Max decided to be as difficult as possible. After all, he needed to find out if the man had character of his own, or had only borrowed courage from his sister.

"Over the last few weeks I have had an opportunity to observe Miss Fraser, and I find her to be a charmingly mannered young lady."

"You observed her carefully, you say?"

Bancroft missed the glimmer of humor in the other man's comment and became more agitated. "I was hardly spying on the girl!" he said, much offended. "It was just that I have been particularly aware of Miss Fraser when we have chanced to encounter each other."

"How splendid."

Finding small help from Max, Bancroft stood up, too restless to be confined to the chair. He tugged his jacket to remove any unsightly wrinkles and then paced in front of Max's desk, occasionally running a hand through his carefully arranged curls, much to their detriment. It was several minutes before he felt composed enough to broach the subject, and then in a burst of energy he spoke, "I should like your permission to pay my addresses to your ward, Miss Amity Fraser."

"That's the ticket, Bancroft," Max applauded.

"For a moment there I thought you might refuse the fence."

"Sir?" he said in bewilderment.

The man certainly was a slow top, Max thought in chagrin. Aloud he said, "As far as I am concerned, you have my permission."

"Good show, sir!" Bancroft cried.

"Before you fall on your knees in gratitude, I should warn you that it will still be up to Amity whether or not she accepts your proposal," Max warned.

"I understand."

"When she arises this morning, I shall acquaint her with your visit. Perhaps you might care to return this afternoon for her answer."

"Would two be convenient?"

"Excellent."

After several more bursts of enthusiasm from Bancroft, Max ushered the man out and returned to the library. He walked to the window overlooking the garden. Placing his boot on the window seat, he rested his arms on his knee, his face thoughtful. He had already given the word to Putnam to send Amity to see him when she came down. Now he debated the best way to approach the subject.

He should be elated that he had found such an eligible party for the girl. It was true, she was an heiress and fair of face, but that did not always mean success in the marriage mart. Though slightly priggish, Bancroft Paige was an exceptional choice. He was reputed to be quite plump in the pocket and had at least two estates that Max knew of. Naturally he would have his man of business check further into his credentials to be certain he was sound. His ward should be delighted that the man had finally come up to scratch. He assumed the blond curls and lean body would be a considerable advantage in helping Amity make her decision.

As her guardian he had finally arranged a suitable match. He wondered why he had been so quick to refuse the other offers; with the exception of General Cuthburton, most had been respectable suitors. In retrospect, he supposed Paige was the best of the lot. It was a shame that he could not like the man better. Over the years he had seen a fair amount of Paige, and he had observed no depth of feeling or love of culture that might have mitigated the overall negative feeling he had for the man. Max found him rather shallow, with a tendency to be slightly self-righteous and pompous. However, in the long run it was not his decision to make. As guardian he had found an eligible suitor for the hand of his ward.

"Good morning, Max," Amity chirped from the doorway.

The girl came into the room like a cloud of butterflies, Max thought inanely. Her dress was a cornflower silk that shimmered in the sunlight as she crossed the carpet. There were soft touches of filmy lace at the rounded neck and wrists, but aside from that, the gown was free of ornamentation. A wide-brimmed straw hat trimmed with small blue flowers was dangling by its ribbons from her hand. The other held a sleek parasol, which matched her dress.

Placing his boot on the floor, Max turned to greet his ward. She came at him in a rush, stumbling over a wrinkle in the carpet, and he caught her in his arms. He was surrounded by the fresh scent of flowers, and for a moment held her against his chest as he drew in the lovely fragrance. She moved and he pushed her upright, crossing his hands behind his back, much too aware of the feel of the girl's body.

"Must I always charge you to enter a room with dignity," he snapped.

"I'm sorry, Max," Amity said, puzzled at his sudden anger since he had just been smiling at her with some fondness. "Putnam told me you wanted to see me, and I didn't want to keep you waiting."

"Well, I appreciate your promptness," Max responded stiffly, moving to stand behind the desk, effectively creating a barrier between himself and his lovely ward. "Please have a seat. I would have a word with you."

Amity sat down on the chair that Paige had so recently vacated. In an unconscious imitation, she too was perched on the edge of the seat, her eyes slightly apprehensive as she stared across the desk. He refused to further duplicate the scene, so he came around to the front of the desk and sat on the corner facing her.

"This morning I had an interview with Bancroft Paige." He could tell by the sudden blink of her eyes that she was aware of the purpose of the man's visit. Surely he hadn't spoken prematurely to the girl. "Did you know he had asked to see me?"

"No, sir," she said, eyes lowered to her lap. "I had reason to believe that he might ask for an interview. He hinted of such the last time he called."

"Are you aware of the subject he wished to discuss?"

"Yes," she whispered, her voice barely audible and a flush burning high on her cheekbones. "I have reason to suspect that he has developed a *tendre* for me."

"Exactly." Max waited, but there were no more words forthcoming. "Confound it, Amity. Must you memorize the pattern of your dress? I'll admit, it is extremely fetching, but I refuse to hold any further conversation with the top of your head."

Amity giggled, and slowly she raised her head so that Max had full benefit of her crystal blue eyes. As always he was fascinated by the clarity of color. Her complexion was glowing, and for a moment he ached to touch her soft cheek. He shook his head, trying to focus on the subject under discussion.

"That's better. Now, then. I am happy to tell you that I have already received several offers for your hand besides the one this morning. I have considered them all carefully and as of this moment feel that Bancroft Paige would be an acceptable suitor."

"Do you like him?" Amity asked.

"More to the point, my dear, is whether you like him."

"He is exceedingly handsome," she admitted. She caught her lower lip between her teeth, her eyes focused inward. "I have found his company pleasurable and his manners are impeccable."

"Do you have some feeling for the man?"

"I do not know," she answered slowly. She blinked rapidly several times and brought her attention back to her guardian. "What sort of feeling?"

"It varies, my dear." By her very confusion Max could tell that her heart was not engaged with Paige, and for some reason that pleased him. He supposed it was because he wished her to make a thoughtful decision, rather than leap to a conclusion as she was wont to do. "Sometimes it is a feeling that you miss the person, or your heart might jump with excitement when you see a certain someone. Do you feel that with Bancroft?"

Amity's nose wrinkled as she concentrated on her feelings. Moments later she shook her head, looking rather wistful. "Truly, Max, I cannot claim to either of those feelings. All I can say is that I am always pleased to see him. He can be very amusing. I enjoy talking to him, and we seem to be friends."

"There is more to marriage than mere friendship," Max said. There was such an aura of innocence that surrounded Amity that he wondered how much awareness she had of the intimacies of married life. "Have any of the gentlemen of your acquaintance made any advances to you? A touch or a stolen kiss?"

"Oh, no, Max. They have treated me with great care," she answered, her eyes wide with sincerity.

That certainly is a sad commentary on modern youth, Max thought dryly. He could not imagine how any virile young man could be in the company of Amity and not try to press a kiss on that wide, lush mouth. The cherry lips were parted now, and the sheen of moisture covering them beckoned irresistibly. He groaned at his wandering thoughts and jerked away from the desk, walking toward the door.

"Bancroft in particular," Amity continued, "has

been most gentlemanly. He treats me very well, as if I were some fragile flower, which at times I find rather amusing. Would you like me to marry him?"

"Heaven forfend, Amity!" Max whirled around and glared at the girl.

"I thought you said you found him an acceptable suitor," Amity argued.

"I am not the one who will be marrying the man! You are the one who must make the decision. As your guardian it is my duty to make sure that any offer made to you would be to your benefit. All I have said is that I find Bancroft Paige acceptable."

"There is little need to shout at me, Max," Amity said, an injured look on her face as she gripped the parasol with both hands. "I am trying to understand what you want me to do."

"My dear, I am sorry for being so contentious," Max said wearily. He did not wish to argue the merits of Bancroft Paige. He wanted Amity to make her decision quickly so that he might get on with his own life, free of her disturbing presence. He drew a deep breath and crossed the room to stand beside her chair. "Please believe me, I have only your best interests at heart. Paige will call on you this afternoon. It is an extremely good offer, and I think you should accept him. Perhaps you do not entertain any strong feelings for him at this point, but once you are married those feelings will come. I think he would make a good husband. He would provide financial security, and he no doubt would cause you little grief," Max said.

"It does not sound very exciting," Amity ventured. Then seeing the smoldering glint in her guardian's eye, she hurried on. "Thank you for your advice, Max. I will think on it. When he comes, I will give him my answer."

After Amity left, Max sat for a long time staring at the books on the shelves without really seeing them. He suspected with his recommendation, Amity would accept Paige's offer. For once the girl was doing what he wanted. He should be jumping for joy, yet he felt only a curious depression. Determined to ride off his ill humor, he stomped off to the stables.

Amity spent her time pacing her bedroom considering what answer to give to Bancroft. As usual Muffin reclined on the striped chaise longue, occasionally opening one or both eyes to consider the restlessness of his mistress. Sometimes as she passed him, she stroked the soft, curly head, and he responded with an unenthusiastic tail wag.

She tried to remind herself of how much she wanted to marry and have a child to love, but somehow that thought did not stir her as it used to. It had become apparent to her that having a baby was not the perfect solution to her loneliness. In her dealings with Max she had discovered the real joy to be found in a friendship with a man. This was such a novel experience for her that she did not understand why she had not suspected it earlier. Her solitary life at Beech House had not prepared her for the contentment she would feel in her relationship with her guardian. She loved talking with Max, sharing ideas, and arguing about books or the latest news; she enjoyed being with him, watching the play of emotions across his face and the special way his eyes lit up in approval. It never had occurred to her that this type of relationship was possible or that she would find it so satisfying. This revolutionary idea was extremely confusing.

For Amity a child had always been the reason for marriage. She was now beginning to understand that the real prize to strive for was to find a person to marry who could love her, and with whom she could share an adult relationship. A child would be a bonus, a gift of celebration of her love for a man. Now she wondered if without that love, her life would be complete.

She liked Bancroft better than any of the other men she had met since her arrival in London. He was handsome, and in her dealings with him he had been kind to her. Was it possible that she might grow to love him? Max wanted her to marry Bancroft, and she did want to please her guardian. He was far more worldly than she, and he seemed to think she would deal well with Bancroft. She knew she must marry. She could not continue to live with her guardian and Lady Grassmere. Especially if Max married Honoria.

With all her heart she wished he would not marry the woman. She loved Max dearly and would have him marry a woman who could bring light and laughter to his life. He had changed much since the day she had arrived at Edgeworth. It had seemed to Amity then that he was little used to laughter, but as the days and weeks passed, he had seemed to view the world more humorously, and his words were less filled with biting sarcasm. There was little laughter in Honoria.

Amity admitted that she did not have a positive opinion about the woman, but it was not just based on her own dealings with her. The more she went

about in society, the more aware Amity was of the
ill feelings others had toward Miss Waterston, and
she was amazed that Max should still think so
highly of the woman. She had come to the conclusion that Honoria was two-faced, showing only sunshine and docility to Max while hiding another side,
which was considerably darker.

Before Amity was brought to Edgeworth, she had
thought only occasionally of Max. Because she did
not know him, she made of him a hero. Now that
she knew him, he was no less a hero, and if he were
suddenly gone from her life, she would miss him
terribly. If he married Honoria, she knew that she
would see little of Max. His bride would take care
of that.

Amity's eyes filled at the very thought, and she
dropped down on the end of the chaise, her hand
unconsciously reaching out to take comfort from
Muffin's nearness. She closed her eyes and placed
her head on the dog's back, listening to the steady
rhythm of his heartbeat.

Muffin snuffled in his sleep, and Amity stroked
his soft hair until he quieted. Then she pushed herself upright, dried her eyes, and considered what
she should do. She had seen the growing attraction
between Betta and Jason Conway. It was apparent
to her that they were falling in love, and she wished
that she felt the strong pull of emotions to guide
her in her decision. All she could do was to listen
to Bancroft's declaration and see if her heart spoke
to her. If she felt she could grow fond of him, then
she would accept him.

Her glance flicked to the clock, and she sighed at
how quickly the time had passed. If she did not

hurry, she would miss lunch and that would surely disappoint Lady Grassmere. She was nervous over the coming interview and had little enthusiasm for conversation. Lady Grassmere was concerned over her silence and kept asking her if she were well. It was almost a relief when Bancroft Paige was announced. Lady Grassmere was well aware of the import of the man's visit, having been primed by Max, so after some general conversation, she excused herself to search for more thread for her needlework. Amity clasped her hands in her lap and waited for Bancroft to speak.

"If I may be permitted to say so, Miss Fraser, you look exceedingly lovely today. Blue becomes you."

Bancroft spoke from the side of the fireplace near where he had been sitting when Lady Grassmere had made her graceful exit. A smile tugged at Amity's mouth, and she wondered if he were going to shout his declaration from such a distance.

"Thank you for your kind words. And may I return the compliment, milord. You are exceedingly well turned out today."

It was true, Amity thought. Bancroft was not as tall as Max and his body was not as muscular, but he wore his clothes with a similar air of sophistication. He knew he was handsome and held himself with arrogance. He was wearing a dark brown jacket and biscuit-colored trousers above highly polished top boots. His shirt was the softest of lawn, and his cravat was tied simply but elegantly. His blond curls were brushed into the popular Windswept, which on him complimented the beauty of his features. Amity thought he looked rather like a cupid with his bow-shaped mouth.

"Have you spoken to your guardian, Miss Fraser?" Bancroft moved several feet closer and leaned negligently against the back of a high-backed chair.

"Yes. This morning." She lowered her eyes so he might not see her amusement at his maneuvering. She felt rather like a dove being stalked by a hawk. "He told me to expect your call."

"I wish to tell you, Miss Fraser, that I admire you greatly." Bancroft's voice came from the far side of the round table in front of the settee on which Amity sat.

"Thank you," she mumbled, knowing her words were inadequate to the occasion, but she could think of nothing intelligent to reply.

"Your manners show excellent background and breeding, Miss Fraser."

"Oh!" The nearness of his voice startled her, and when she raised her eyes, she was amazed at how quickly he had moved, for he now stood directly beside her.

"Oh, Miss Fraser, will you do me the kind honor of accepting my regard for you by saying you will be my wife?"

At this ardent declaration, Bancroft threw himself down on one knee in front of her. Although Amity had been expecting this eventuality, she was surprised that she felt only an urge to giggle. For the moment her heart seemed to be indicating little that was useful.

"Come, your lordship, have done with this drama," she said briskly. At his look of affronted dignity, she lowered her voice to a more coaxing tone. "Marriage is a serious business, and I would deal fairly with you. Come, sit beside me where we can talk more easily."

She patted the cushion beside her and smiled sweetly into his face. Though annoyed that his well-staged proposal was not going as smoothly as expected, Bancroft was not impervious to the enchantment. Grumbling low in his throat, he stood up and brushed the creases from his trousers before seating himself beside her.

"I must tell you first, that I am sensible of the singular honor you do me by seeking my hand in marriage." She was relieved that her words had such a salubrious effect on his bearing. "I like you very well, and I could accept your offer if I were convinced we would suit."

"How generous you are, Miss Fraser."

"We are much too formal for this occasion. Perhaps I might call you Bancroft, and you would consent to call me Amity," she suggested, her blue eyes twinkling merrily.

"It would be my honor, Amity."

Bancroft beamed at her. He had taken possession of her hand and was patting it with the same attention as one might in consoling a child. She felt a little less awkward now that they were sitting side by side.

"I wish to be totally honest with you," Amity said, gulping slightly in her nervousness. Finally she blurted out the words that had been bothering her, "As much as I admire you, Bancroft, I cannot truly tell you that I am in love with you."

"Love?" Bancroft looked surprised at her words. "But I did not expect that, my dear. After all, until we are married, it would be strange indeed if you should entertain such feelings. Love is based on many qualities, and quite naturally these would be brought on by the, shall we say, the intimacies of married life."

"Oh," Amity said, flushing in confusion.

"At this time I would hope you might admire me and think of me as a friend. After we are married, you will find that the feelings we have for each other will grow in depth. You do not find me repugnant?" he asked jokingly.

"Oh, never that, Bancroft," Amity cried. She could not believe she was making such a hash of things. She breathed deeply and held her breath, slowly releasing it as her composure was restored. "I like you very well."

"I can offer you financial security and an impeccable name. I am not one to dally in the clubs or fritter away my funds in gambling hells. I do not approve of loose morals, so you need have no fear that I will embarrass you in that area. I do not consider myself a demanding person, and you would be free to conduct yourself much as you are used to," he concluded.

"You will obviously make a very good husband," Amity said with all sincerity. "Are you really certain that I will make you a good wife?"

"Since the first night I met you, I have been aware of your quality, my dear," Bancroft said. "Although at first I was slightly taken aback by your hair, I find I have become used to it. You have learned to confine it in a most becoming manner. Your manners in company are excellent. Your sense of style and your ease of conversation are unexceptionable. Always conscious of my obligations to society, I have seen nothing in your behavior to suggest you would not be acceptable in all quarters."

"Thank you, Bancroft," Amity said. She smiled wistfully, wishing somehow that his words had been more loverlike, but then she supposed that too would come more easily after marriage.

"Do you see any impediment to our betrothal, my dear?" he asked.

Amity was silent for a moment, wondering how she should broach one area that troubled her. She wondered if he had told his sister that he planned to offer for her. She wished she had had more of an opportunity to get to know Ophelia. When she was around the woman, she sensed a slight disapproval, but perhaps that was her way. Ophelia and Bancroft were very close, and it would be difficult if the woman did not like her.

"I do not see an impediment, but I do have one concern. That is, I worry that your s-sister might not approve," she said, stumbling slightly over her words. "How will Ophelia receive this news?"

"It is my fond hope that she will be gratified by my choice."

Amity noticed an expression of uneasiness shadow his face and wondered if Ophelia had already verbalized some objection. "I know you are very fond of your sister, and I would hate to think she might not approve. I will be frank in saying that I have not had a loving family around me as a child, and I would much regret if my marrying you created a rift in your relationship."

"Ah, my dear. I can see you will make a wonderful helpmate in attempting to smooth the course of our lives together," Bancroft said, smiling benignly at her. "Ophelia may have some slight reservation at this point, but it is only because she does not see you in the same light that I do. Once you two have more time together, I know you will become good friends."

"Might I offer a suggestion, Bancroft?" At his nod she continued, "Perhaps you might bring your sister to tea next week. Then she would have a chance to judge more clearly if I would make a suitable wife."

"That's a splendid idea. Would Monday be too soon?" he asked eagerly.

"That would be fine," Amity said. "If she approves, then I will feel that we are really destined to be married. Once we have her approval, then I will be happy to accept your kind and generous offer."

"Oh, my dear. You have made me extremely happy," Bancroft said, raising her hand to his lips and dropping a light kiss on the back of it. "I am sure Ophelia will be delighted, just as I am."

"Thank you, Bancroft. Most especially for your patience."

"In light of your decision, perhaps you would not consider me too forward if I were to request one kiss as a token of our coming betrothal." His face was grave, and his eyes held an intensity that left Amity quite breathless.

She was startled at the request and lowered her eyes in confusion. She had never received a kiss from a lover, but since Max's mention of the subject, found she was curious as to what feelings it might engender. She was not brave enough to speak; she could only nod her head in agreement.

Bancroft placed his hands on her shoulders, careful not to wrinkle her gown. He turned her toward him, and Amity found her heart beating at a terrifying rate. She closed her eyes as he bent his head and waited. Cool, dry lips pressed hers.

For Amity the kiss was pleasurable. There was a sweetness to the caress, a promise of kindness and security. She felt safe in Bancroft's embrace, and she sighed with contentment.

"I assume, I may wish you happy," Max's voice was snapped from the doorway.

Bancroft released Amity so suddenly that she almost fell off the settee. The embarrassed gentleman leaped to his feet, standing awkwardly beside her. How poor of Max to interrupt such a blissful experience, she thought in annoyance. Before Bancroft could stammer a reply, she smoothed her skirts and raised ingenuous eyes to her guardian.

"Good afternoon, Max. Won't you join us?" she said, hoping she sounded cool, although her pulses were still racing at his sudden appearance. "Bancroft was bidding me good-bye."

"Forever?" came the lugubrious response.

"Naturally not. He will be calling to take me for a drive tomorrow." Turning to Bancroft, she was relieved to see that he had regained his composure. "Shall we say two?"

"It will be my pleasure," he agreed. Then before the startled Max could do anything more than wish him good day, Bancroft had exited the room.

"Devil take it, Amity." Max stormed across the carpet to glare down at the gently smiling girl. "Have you accepted the man or haven't you?"

"I have not exactly accepted him," she began,

dropping her gaze at sight of the glittering green eyes that threatened mayhem at the very least.

"Then how dare you let him lay hands on you. He will have a thorough disgust of you, and your reputation will be in shreds," Max sneered.

"It was only a kiss, Max. He did not even muss my gown."

"If that is your criterion for modest behavior, you are well out there, my girl." Max dug his hands in his hair, though he mentally acknowledged the fact that he would much prefer to throttle the girl. "Many a deb has found her virtue gone without the slightest damage done to her apparel. In fact, some prefer it that way," he finished crudely, wanting to shock her.

"Seems most uncomfortable" was the irrepressible Amity's reply. "Besides, Max, it was only an experiment."

"Good Lord!" Max cried, throwing himself in a chair across from the settee. "What will you be up to next, I wonder?"

"I was curious." He gave her a lowering frown, and she knew he was none too pleased with her comment. "I have tentatively accepted his offer. I think that I might learn to love him, and I thought perhaps if he kissed me, I would discover for certain whether I could entertain deeper feelings for him."

"And can you?" he asked.

"Yes, I think so," she said, her face thoughtful as she recalled the event. "I liked it very much."

"I see," Max said quietly. "And perhaps you might explain what you meant about tentatively accepting his offer."

"I have told him that the only impediment to our

marrying is his sister. I do not think that Ophelia approves of me, Max."

"Is that so important?" he asked in surprise.

"She would be living in the same house with us. Bancroft is terribly fond of her, and it would be hurtful if my marrying him should end their relationship." Amity sighed heavily. "When I was growing up, my parents did not approve of me. I do not want to repeat that experience."

Looking across at the sad expression of his ward, Max wanted nothing more than to assure her that Ophelia Paige would love her. He wished he could erase the loneliness she had felt as a child and felt guilty that he also had contributed to that feeling of rejection. Wishing he could go to her and hold her against all the hurts of the world, he tightened his hands on the arms of the chair and spoke quietly. "I think you show good sense, poppet."

"Thank you, sir," she said, dimpling prettily. "I have invited Bancroft to bring his sister, Ophelia, to tea on Monday. If she does approve, then we will announce our engagement."

Max noted Amity's glowing face and felt a sadness creep into his heart. Though he might not think Bancroft the most exciting of men, he was eminently suitable, and it seemed that his ward might even be falling in love with the man. Soon he could return to the joys of a bachelor household. Surprisingly the thought did little to alleviate his feeling of depression.

Chapter Nine

"Some punch, Honoria?" Max asked as they strolled off the dance floor.

"That would be splendid," she admitted, waving her fan languidly before her face. "I must admit that it is extremely warm in here this evening. You would think Theresa would know better than to have such a squeeze this late in the season."

After a glass of punch, they wandered around talking to friends until they reached the open doors to the terrace. By mutual consent they stepped outside, where the temperature was only marginally cooler. Max inhaled deeply, refreshed by the clean air, not heavy with the scent of mingling perfume as the stale atmosphere inside.

"You must feel quite carefree this evening. Where are Lady Grassmere and your little ward?"

It amused Max that Honoria had taken to calling Amity his "little" ward, since the girl was a good head taller than she. When he had arranged for Honoria to be Amity's mentor, he had hoped that they would become good friends. He still did not quite understand what had gone wrong in their relationship, but he suspected that neither woman liked the other. In his presence there had been nothing except the most polite of exchanges; however, the general lack of warmth and intimacy between them convinced him of the true state of their feelings.

In truth, Amity had never said an unkind word about Honoria. Granted, she had not been fulsome in her praises, and that was a fair indication of the extent of her friendship with the older woman. Amity was nothing if not enthusiastic about her friends and was more inclined to discuss her relationship with her abigail, Betta, than any commerce she had with Honoria.

"Cousin Hester was feeling unwell, and Amity thought they might both benefit from an evening at home," Max replied. "I have been pleased that her come-out has been such a success."

"Yes, most have accepted her without question, thanks to your sponsorship. I saw her last night at the Duchess of Landglower's affair. Amity looked quite charming."

"She has gained some sophistication since her arrival in London, my dear," Max said, his eyes alight with pleasure. "Naturally I owe much of this polish to your credit for being such an example of the ideal in feminine perfection."

"Why, thank you, Max," Honoria said, fluttering her eyes coyly from behind the modestly raised fan. "I have, of course, tried to help the sweet child where I could. One can see the enormous amount of money she has spent on her wardrobe by the elegant gown she was wearing last evening. Perhaps it may have been a trifle sophisticated for a girl of her age, but I am sure no one will think that she is too fast."

Max cocked an eyebrow at the comment, but when he glanced at Honoria, she raised guileless eyes to him. He turned the words over in his mind and wondered if she was being intentionally critical. He led her down the stone steps to the formal garden, his mind busy with the puzzle.

As he looked back over the past weeks, he had to admit that Honoria had made many such comments about Amity. They were always thinly disguised as compliments, but there was a knife edge of disparagement implied. Now that he thought about it, although Amity had never said a word against her, Honoria had been constantly critical of his ward. It was borne in on him, that it was almost as if Honoria was the one who had taken a dislike to Amity, and she was doing all she could to denigrate her in Max's eyes. He found it difficult to believe this since he had always thought of Honoria as the epitome of gracious, ladylike behavior.

Max was oblivious to the moonlight playing romantically on the garden paths. He walked beside Honoria, his mind intent on his confusion, until finally he was reminded of her presence by a gentle tug on his sleeve.

"Would you mind if we sat for a moment, Max? My poor feet are quite worn from dancing."

"My apologies, my dear," Max said.

He was immediately contrite that he should have been so little aware of her discomfort. Taking out his handkerchief, he rubbed it over the stone bench and then held her hand as she daintily positioned herself on the seat. Staring down at her, he was conscious of her beauty. The moonlight gave a metallic sheen to the blond curls and a softness to her white skin. Tonight he was less affected by her loveliness than usual, perhaps because his mind had been questioning whether he knew her as well as he assumed. Troubled by his disloyal thoughts, he sat down on the bench and turned to gaze at her intently.

"Do you like Amity?" he asked, surprised at his own words.

"Why, Max, what a question," Honoria said, waving her fan briskly as an indication of her discomposure. "Of course, I am extremely fond of your little ward."

"I have wondered and felt some disquiet." Max pursed his lips, debating how he could find an answer to his confusion. "I suspect a coolness between you two, and I am concerned that Amity has given you reason to feel hostility toward her."

"Hostility, Max? Why, I don't know what to make of your words," Honoria said. She stared at him with injured eyes, then lowered her lids, and bent her head. She closed her fan with a brittle snap and tapped the sticks against the palm of her hand. She was silent for several moments, then spoke, her words barely audible in the quiet night air. "Oh, Max, it is only that sometimes I worry others may take advantage of your goodness of spirit."

Max felt a tug of amusement at her words. He had never considered that he had a goodness of spirit, quite the contrary in fact. He generally arranged things selfishly so that he was put to the least amount of disorder in his life.

"Come now, my dear," he said. "No one has taken advantage of my goodwill."

"If you say so," she said, sounding not at all convinced.

His forehead wrinkled at her tone, and he narrowed his eyes in contemplation of her still bent head. "I can see you are troubled about something, Honoria. Please do me the courtesy of telling me your thoughts so that I may persuade you that there is nothing to worry about." As she remained silent, Max felt annoyance at her reticence. "Is it Amity? Has she committed some unpardonable breach of propriety?"

Honoria raised her head, and her eyes were wide with apprehension. He smiled as she batted her lashes in a pretty picture of hesitation. At his encouragement, she brushed out her skirts, then crossed her hands in her lap, and straightened her shoulders bravely.

"I have been so hesitant to speak," she began.

"Do you see me as some kind of ogre?" he chided her jokingly.

"Of course not, Max. You know how highly I regard you. It is only that it is difficult sometimes to know when to tell tales. I would not say a word now, except for my concern for darling Amity."

"I appreciate your situation, Honoria. Please continue."

"It was several weeks ago when I chanced to see your ward. I was driving with Percy to see our man of business. The street was crowded, and our carriage had come to a stop when I looked up and saw Amity, all alone, in conversation with a man."

"She was alone?" Max asked in surprise.

Honoria swallowed as if hesitant to answer. "Well, yes, except for her abigail. I naturally assumed Lady Grassmere would be nearby, but though I searched the street, I could find no evidence of her presence."

"I see. So Amity and this young man were in conversation." At Honoria's nod he asked, "Who was the gentleman?"

"It was no one of my acquaintance." She hesitated for a moment and then blurted out, "In fact, the man was no gentleman at all. He was a soldier."

"A soldier!" Max snapped out the words, his mind instantly recalling the references of the servants to a soldier.

"Oh, Max, I would have spoken immediately if I had thought there was anything unusual going on. Amity is forever speaking to people, persons quite beneath notice in most cases. But, of course, it is her habit, and although I have spoken to her many times, she has stubbornly refused to change her ways. But in any case I assumed it was only a chance meeting between the handsome young man and your ward."

"He was young?" Max asked, his brow furrowed in mounting anger.

"Yes. About the same age as Amity. A very muscular sort of man with a dark-tanned face. I can well imagine how a young girl might be caught under the spell of a man in uniform. It would seem most romantic to an untutored girl such as Amity."

"A chance meeting does not a romance make," Max answered huffily. "I shall speak to her immediately. I am well aware of her penchant for speaking to everyone. She is so very trusting, you know, and has little knowledge of the evils of the city."

"That is why I have been so concerned," Honoria said, her voice slightly unctuous. "I was intending to speak to her again on that very subject, but I quite forgot. I would have thought no more about the incident, except on Tuesday last, I was astonished to discover Amity in the park with the very same young man."

"What?" Max shouted, leaping to his feet in his astonishment.

"Softly, my dear. I am sure you would not want this contretemps common knowledge." Honoria patted the bench, and he reseated himself, holding his temper under tight rein.

"Honoria, I do not mean to sound censorious, but I feel you should have spoken to me earlier about this matter."

"Please don't be angry with me, Max." She fumbled in her reticule for a lacy handkerchief and raised it to her eyes in her distress. "I was torn between my duty to you and my friendship with your little ward."

"I beg of you, my dear, not to become distressed. I should never have spoken so harshly to you. You are in no way at fault. Just tell me exactly what you saw." In truth, Max wanted to shake the information out of his companion and was appalled that he should be so little caring of her sensibilities. Fury at Amity's behavior and concern for her welfare vied for precedence in his mind. He waited with little patience for Honoria to continue.

"I was walking in the park near your town house with Roger Danforth when I looked up and to my astonishment your ward was sitting on a bench talking to her soldier. He was no longer in uniform, but I recognized him immediately. Amity was so deep in conversation that she did not see me, but I almost wish she had. Then I might have had an opportunity to warn her concerning such behavior." She reached out and patted Max consolingly on the arm. "I know what hopes you have for the girl in regard to Bancroft Paige. Both he and his sister are sticklers for all the niceties of etiquette. If word came to their ears concerning Amity's indiscreet meeting with a young man in a public park, I cannot imagine what might happen."

"I can. It would put paid to her chances," Max answered grimly. "*Entre nous*, my dear, Amity and Bancroft have reached an understanding. Not an official betrothal, mind. They feel they must wait for Ophelia's approval."

"Oh, Max, that is splendid news!" Honoria cried. Her face wore a smile of unusual warmth, and she reached for his hand, squeezing it in her excitement. "I am so thrilled for dear, little Amity. She must be over the moon with elation at her good fortune."

"I suppose so," Max said gloomily. "I was assuming all would be successful, but with this new folly one wonders if she has lost her wits entirely. A soldier," he snorted in disgust.

"You mustn't be too harsh with the child," Honoria said, her voice soft with appeal. "She is new to the ways of society and has much to learn. I am just pleased that you now will have an opportunity to warn her. Ever since I saw her with the young

man, I have been in a quandary over what action
to take to protect her from her own folly."

"Telling me was the proper action, my dear. I
shall definitely get to the bottom of this." Max's
firmly closed lips and grim features indicated that
the subject was closed and his ward would have
much to answer for her actions. Returning to the
ballroom, he noted the bouncing step of Honoria
and realized she was obviously relieved to have finally confessed her guilty secrets. Amity must be
made aware of how good a friend she had in Honoria. Thank heaven that he understood women, he
thought in relief.

When Max returned home, it was late and both
Lady Grassmere and Amity had retired. He debated waking the girl, but he was so angry with
her that he was afraid he would handle things
poorly. The thought that she had been participat-
ing in secret meetings with some unknown soldier
infuriated him. How could she be so stupid as to
risk her reputation in some light flirtation?

He entered the library and poured himself a large
brandy, sipping the liquor without conscious
awareness of its fine quality. Throwing himself into
his high-backed chair, he stretched out his legs,
prying each shoe off with the toe of the other. He
propped his feet up on a footstool and once more
considered the problem of Amity.

Granted, she was impetuous and childlike in her
curiosity and enthusiasm, but he had never felt she
was either immodest or flirtatious. She was friendly
to all the men who flocked around her, but he had
noticed that she never permitted any of the men to
make advances to her. In fact, he had heard her

scold them when they praised her with the flowery compliments they were accustomed to use. She treated them all with the avuncular affection generally reserved for younger, and not necessarily brighter, brothers. It seemed out of character that this practical miss should have fallen afoul of some soldier with immoral intentions; Amity was far too honorable to be involved in some tawdry liaison. Despite Honoria's interpretation, Max felt that there had to be some other explanation.

There was much going on in his household that he felt needed clarification. He was still chagrined that he had not been able to discover what a piglet was doing loose in his foyer and what had been going on in the garden storeroom. It had been several days before he was able to visit the area, since he wished to avoid any appearance that he was snooping in his own garden. When he finally went to the storeroom, the only evidence that he could discover of any animals' occupancy was a strong aroma of the barnyard and a chair minus several mouthfuls of stuffing.

Although this might have been enough to worry him, he had noticed other peculiarities in the running of his household. Most of the servants employed on his various estates had been affiliated with his family for years. However, over the past several weeks, he had noticed an increasing number of new faces in and around the town house and the stables. Despite the fact he had never paid much attention to his household staff, he could swear there was an ever changing supply of strange men in his employ.

Amity's arrival in his life had turned his orderly

bachelor existence topsy-turvy. Perhaps he might have been more zealous in his investigations, but he had to admit that in some ways there were benefits to the reformation of his life. From one day to the next he had no way of predicting what novelty he would find in his household; instead of the boredom he had been prone to, he discovered he awakened in the morning with anticipation of what the day might offer. There was an atmosphere that pervaded the town house, a feeling of lightness and joy that had been totally absent before Amity flew into his life. It was apparent in the smiling faces of the servants and in an air of happiness that crept into each room, like the bowls of flowers the girl was forever arranging.

However, after his discussion with Honoria, Max knew that he would need to determine exactly what the girl was up to. He could not close his eyes to the possibility that her impetuous nature might have catapulted her into some sort of trouble.

The first thing he needed was information. Although he could ask Putnam, he was not positive the starchy man would give him satisfactory answers to his questions. All of the servants had become slaves to Amity's slightest wish. They fair doted on the minx and despite the fact their first allegiance was to Max, he suspected they would protect her from his wrath if put to the test. Besides, he would much prefer to find out on his own and deal with it himself.

In particular Max was determined to communicate directly with Amity's soldier. If the man somehow were taking advantage of her trusting nature,

Max fully intended to teach him a very painful lesson.

Putnam was not to be approached, so Max's next possibility for information was his own valet. The old man was always aware of the goings on in the household and, less astute than the butler, might not be aware of Max's gentle probing if handled correctly. Unfortunately he would have to wait until morning to question Wilberforce, since several years ago he had told the old man he was quite capable of finding his own way to bed. On that thought he downed the last of his brandy and left the library for his bed.

After a good night's sleep, Max was awake on all counts when Wilberforce threw back the draperies to announce the arrival of the day.

" 'Tis a fine morning, your lordship," the little man chirped. "Did you have a good evening, sir?"

"It was the usual crush, but the wine at least was tolerable." Max's voice was muffled as he slipped the nightshirt over his head. "Was Lady Grassmere feeling better?"

"She had an early night of it, so I should imagine she'll feel more the thing this morning. She's no longer young, milord, and she's been out quite a bit with Miss Amity."

"I assume Miss Amity retired early. I had hoped to have a few words with her last night," he said as he made his morning ablutions and returned to the bedroom.

"She read for some time in the library, but was not up much past ten of the clock. I think the fawn trousers, milord," Wilberforce said, indicating the clothes already laid out. "And perhaps a waterfall?" he asked, holding up a snowy cravat hopefully.

"Just something simple," Max suggested, easing into the dark superfine jacket.

"As you say, milord."

Wilberforce sniffed his disapproval and busied himself straightening the room, his face wearing a look of injury. Timing his actions perfectly, he appeared at Max's side with the jewelry box just as his master completed the last of his dressing. Max extracted a garnet ring and a heavily carved gold ring, then busied himself with the alignment of his watch chain.

Keeping his head bent and his voice slightly bored, Max asked abruptly, "Will Miss Fraser be meeting with the soldier today?"

"Aye, milord, 'tis Tuesday," Wilberforce answered without any sign that the question was unusual. He closed the jewelry box and returned it to the dressing room.

While the man was gone, Max congratulated himself on the inspired guess, but immediately composed his expression to one of disinterest. Luckily for the valet's peace of mind, he did not see the calculation in the green eyes of his master when he returned.

"The ivory walking stick, Wilberforce," Max requested. When his valet handed it to him, he tapped the knobby top against his cheek, his eyebrows furrowed in question. "I must be aging rapidly, old man. I have forgotten what Miss Amity said as to time and place."

"Never say, milord. You're looking younger by the day," the valet argued. He scratched the sparse

white hair on his head, then smiled in triumph. "As
I recollect, it's the park at half after one of the
clock."

Max was afraid of putting the wind up the little man with any more questions. He assumed by
the vaguely waving hand of the servant that the
park in question was the one only two blocks from
the town house. He thanked the valet and strolled
from the room, a wolfish smile on his face. Outside
the town house his eyes took on the gleam of the
hunter as he considered his plans. He would wander off to his club and later in the day take a much-
needed bit of exercise.

Just after lunch Max strolled through the gates
of the park, his eyes flickering sharply around the
area. If he knew his girl, she would be on the less
frequented paths, hidden from eyes that might recognize her and report her activities. Pulling his
beaver hat low over his eyes, Max moved to the
first path that cut to the left along the more over-
grown sections of the park. He appeared to stroll
without purpose, his ivory walking stick swinging
loosely in his hand, but in actual fact he was quar-
tering the area in search of his quarry. Soon his
perseverance was rewarded.

Amity sat on a bench in the sun. She was wearing a mint-green muslin dress and perched on her
red curls was a straw hat with a darker green ribbon tied in a bow against her cheek. Beside her was
the neatly dressed abigail, and the ever present
Muffin was sprawled at her feet. Leaning against a
tree not far from Amity, Max smiled at the pretty
picture she made. He was not certain what he had

expected to find, but it was definitely not this pastoral scene of contentment.

A quick glance at his watch told him he was in good time to observe his ward, and he leaned against the trunk of a tree, satisfied for the moment in observing her. He felt no guilt in spying on her; after all, he was responsible for her protection. His patience was rewarded, for soon she was joined by a young man who walked with the jaunty air of a soldier.

Max's eyes focused on the darkly handsome face of the man, and rage such as he had never felt almost sent him catapulting out of the cover of trees. How dare he accost Amity! Max wanted nothing so much as to horsewhip the man who dared consider his ward a fit prospect for some shabby dalliance. A slight movement caught his eye and, at the sight of the empty sleeve pinned to his jacket, reason calmed the whirling tide of Max's anger.

Why hadn't Honoria mentioned the soldier had only one arm, instead of dwelling on the fact that the man was so handsome and muscular? Now that Max looked more closely, he was able to note that the quality of the clothing and the manner of the man were more suited to a servant than some besotted lover. In fact, it was blindingly apparent that the man was barely cognizant of Amity, but was thoroughly besotted by his ward's abigail. Surely Honoria could have checked her suspicions before she accused Amity of a gross impropriety.

"Devil take all women!" Max muttered as he left the comfort of the tree to approach the little group. The threesome was much too deep in conversation to notice his arrival, but the faithful Muffin raised his head and growled a semblance of a greeting. At the sound Amity's eyes opened in astonishment.

"Max!" she called in surprise. Her face glowed with welcome, untinged by any sign of guilty distress.

"Greetings, poppet," Max said, bowing to the party.

"Come let me make you known to our good friend, Jason Conway." Amity made the introductions and smiled as her guardian shook hands with Jason, each man eyeing the other warily.

"I was looking for you, my dear," Max said as his ward eyed him questioningly. "I thought we might sit in the sunshine and have a comfortable coze."

"What a lovely idea," she said. "Mr. Conway was just leaving, but perhaps I might beg a favor, and he could accompany Betta back to the town house."

"It would be my pleasure, miss," Jason said, jumping at the opportunity. With alacrity he helped the blushing abigail to her feet, then tipped his hat in a jaunty salute. "Your servant, Miss Fraser. Your lordship."

Max watched as the one-armed man leaned solicitously over the little abigail as he led her back along the path. He turned to Amity and had to grin at her deep sigh of contentment as she followed the disappearing figures, her gaze misty with vicarious enjoyment. Max cleared his throat and immediately she turned to face him, obviously chagrined to have been so caught up in her romantic fancies.

"I'm sorry, Max," she said. "I was just pleased that Betta could have more of a chance to visit with her young man. She doesn't see as much of him as she would like."

"Don't tell me you're setting up as a match-maker," Max drawled, sitting down on the bench beside the laughing girl.

"He's a wonderful man and just perfect for Betta. I think he will declare himself soon, now that his prospects have improved," she answered smugly.

"Perhaps you might enlighten me as to who this young man is and how you have become acquainted with him," Max said. His tone was light, but Amity noticed the hint of purpose behind his words. "In fact, my charming baggage, you might consider telling me about the additional servants in the household, not to mention the goat and the ever-so-adorable piglets."

"Oh," said Amity, her eyes widening in surprise at the extent of his knowledge.

"Indeed, my dear." Max leaned against the back of the bench and folded his arms across his chest.

By his attitude Amity was conscious that he was determined to wait until she had fully explained, and, gulping once, she nodded, acknowledging that it was time to open her budget. Slowly she began with her meeting with Jason and the plan she and Betta had concocted to help the returning soldiers. He listened with attention, only occasionally inter-jecting a question.

"You have certainly been busy since your arrival in London. And all the time I thought you were gadding about shopping." Max shook his head in amazement. Amity was running some sort of char-ity rig to find jobs for returning soldiers, while most fashionable ladies of the ton were unaware that there was even a need for such action.

"I did go shopping in the beginning, Max," she

argued. "But once I gathered my wardrobe, there was little to do. As you know, I was actively involved in the running of Beech House, and I had begun to feel useless here in town. Now I have much with which to occupy myself. There is always someone in need of a job, or. . . ."

"Don't tell me," Max said, rolling his eyes to the heavens. "There is always someone who needs a home."

She giggled at his expression, then sobered and spoke quite seriously. "I am sorry to have caused you any concern, Max. I would have told you, but I was afraid you might not have approved of my enterprise, and I did so want to be useful."

"Never fear, poppet. I probably shouldn't approve, but, I have to admit, it pleases me greatly to find you have such a generous heart." He watched the flush of color rise in her cheeks at his words. He was used to the fact that she was a beauty, but there was an almost incandescent glow to her skin that quite took his breath away. He shook his head to dispel the magic he felt in her presence. "I think I am aware of most of your startling machinations, but I would still like to understand what has been going on in my storeroom."

"I forgot that part," Amity admitted sheepishly. "It was really Jason's idea. Not to use the garden storeroom. I fear that was something that I hit upon."

"Just give me the straight of it, girl, or we'll be here until winter sets in," Max said dryly.

"Yes, sir. Jason mentioned that some of the soldiers wanted to start a farm. It would provide food for those really in need and a place for some of the injured to go. I suggested to Jason that he locate a likely property, and when he had discovered one not too far from London, I instructed Henderson, my man of business, to purchase it as an investment. The men agreed to the proposition, once I was able to set up a system whereby they could pay off the loan and eventually own the farm themselves."

"Devil you say!" Max was stunned at the businesslike attitude of his ward. "It was my understanding that Henderson was the one making all the decisions on behalf of your estate. Now I begin to wonder."

"In the beginning that was true, Max, but as I grew older, I began to take an active role in the management of the estate. Henderson trusts my judgment now, and is more than willing to accept my orders."

"It has become apparent to me that the vast store of knowledge I had concerning women has been sorely tested by my meeting with you," Max said. He shook his head in bewilderment and grimaced at his ward's tinkling laughter. "Continue if you please," he said sourly.

"Well, after I purchased Lady Guinevere," she said, grinning in remembrance of the pathetic mare, "it occurred to me that I might keep my eyes open for other animals in need of a home. So when I chanced to discover a sow, I bought her and placed her in the garden storeroom until Jason could send someone to retrieve her. I had not counted on the fact that she would litter, and then, of course, I did not want her moved so soon after her confinement."

"Naturally not. It would offend her sensibilities, I am sure."

Amity's eyes sparkled with humor at his bantering words. "Mrs. Putnam didn't mind the ducks, but was not best pleased when I bought the goat. I am afraid it damaged one of the chairs being stored there, but I am quite willing to have the repairs taken out of my allowance."

"I suspect I can stand the expense as my part in this unorthodox project. Did you send all the animals to the farm?"

"Yes and I am happy to report they are thriving. Even Lady Guinevere looks better."

"There was no possibility, short of death, that she could have looked worse," Max drawled. Then in an abrupt change of subject, he asked, "How do you think Bancroft will react to your enterprise?"

For the first time in their discussion, Amity looked slightly uneasy. "I don't know. I would hope that he would consider it a worthwhile cause. After all, the soldiers fought for the freedom of England, Max. It is only right that they not be left in desperate straits now that we no longer have use for them."

"I would agree, poppet, but then I am not the man you are to marry," he commented. "No need to look so grim, Amity. I have the feeling you could convince anyone of the rightness of your actions. Come along home. All this fresh air is exhausting."

Amity took his arm and tried to appear as usual, but his words had left a feeling of gloom deep in her heart. She had not really considered what would happen to the soldiers once she married. Although she hoped that Bancroft might look on her activities as worthy, she suspected he might not be well pleased. She had noticed that most of the fashionable set preferred their good works in the form of donations and disdained anything that might bring them personally into the sphere of those they wished to help.

Amity, for all the loneliness of her early life, was quite used to doing much as she pleased. She had not considered the fact that once she married, she would be responsible for her actions to another person, who might not have the same ideas that she did. In her dealings with Bancroft she had never found him unreasonable, but then she had never really challenged him. She knew he was a proper stickler for the proprieties, and although he appeared easygoing, she suspected he might become quite angry if she did not conform to what he considered was genteel behavior. She considered her actions commensurate with the actions of a lady. But would Bancroft?

Chapter Ten

"Now, Amity, be sure to keep your hat on," warned Hester. "I would feel far happier if I thought you would actually use that fetching parasol you are carrying. The sun is hot and I fear you will come back looking like one of those bizarre natives from the colonies."

"Never fear, Lady Grassmere, we will be lucky to even see the sun on this gloomy day," Amity said as she peered anxiously out the front door at the lowering skies. "You mustn't worry, and take full advantage of my absence by curling up with that new novel I saw you sneaking into the house."

"Hush, Amity," Hester said, her face flaming with embarrassment. "What would the servants think if they heard such talk?"

"They would think you were an eminently sweet lady, just as I do." She kissed the wrinkled cheek and with a wave of her hand skipped down the stairs to the waiting curricle. She accepted Max's assistance into the carriage with a few words of greeting to Lewis, the tiger, who stood holding the horses.

Max waited while she settled her skirts and put up her parasol for the benefit of Lady Grassmere, who stood anxiously in the doorway. He picked up the reins, and Lewis climbed up behind as they started away from the town house at an extremely sedate pace. He appreciated Amity's silence while he tooled his way through the streets. The grays were new and still highly strung, and he needed full concentration to control them in the traffic. Once on the open road, he relaxed and turned to his ward.

"You are looking particularly charming on this dreary day," he said, taking in her toilette with a comprehensive glance.

Amity's dress was a delightfully simple white muslin, banded at the neckline and the edge of the puffed sleeves with satin the exact color of her hair. The sash was the same color and tied beneath her breasts with the ends fluttering down to the hem of her skirt. A cluster of peacock feathers was nestled in the ribbon that circled the crown of her wide-brimmed white straw hat. The opened parasol was the color of her red hair and was lined in white. All in all, she was a charming picture of elegance.

"One must be optimistic, Max. After all, you planned a picnic and I wished to dress for the occasion. It is my hope that the sun shall break through the cloud cover yet."

As if on cue, the sun shyly peeked from behind the blanket of clouds, getting stronger by the minute. Amity crowed her delight and Max tipped his hat in return.

"Where are we heading?" she asked.

"I thought out beyond Greenwich. There's a nice walking lane near the river."

"And to what particular event do I owe this great honor of an entire afternoon of your exalted presence?"

"I was feeling rather restless and selfishly thought it would be an excellent excuse not to be tied up with my man of business. Besides, it occurred to me that in two days' time, you will be a properly betrothed young lady and have little time for your guardian. Soon you will be too busy with plans for your wedding to enjoy just a carefree afternoon," he finished quietly.

"It's true," she said, her tone less than enthusiastic. "If Ophelia approves, Bancroft wishes to make the announcement immediately. I had really not thought beyond the betrothal, but there are probably endless details to planning a wedding."

Amity was silent for the remainder of the ride, noticing little of the passing scenery. She awakened from her reverie when Max reined in the grays and looked around her in wonderment.

"I hope you approve," he said as he helped her out of the carriage.

"How could I not?" She skipped forward a few paces, then hurried back, her face alight with pleasure. "It is beautiful here. The river in London is so full of noisome things that I find little enjoyment in viewing it. This is how it should look."

"Well don't just stand there like some fashionable fribble," Max said, arms akimbo. "You would have it that we sneak off on our own, so unless you carry something, I shall be all day playing donkey. Lewis"—he flashed a grin at his tiger—"must remain abandoned with the horses."

Amity laughed and accepted the armful of blankets and cushions, while Max carried an enormous picnic hamper. They walked up the lane until they found a particularly lovely spot beside the river. Together they spread out the blankets amid much laughter as to the perfect position. Finally they were satisfied and Amity dropped to the ground, tucking her legs beneath her muslin skirts in a naturally graceful gesture. She watched with pleasure as Max delved into the hamper and began to unload the food.

"Mrs. Putnam must think we are planning to be gone this sennight," she said. "Chicken and ham. Oh, Max, are those cherry tarts? I vow they are my very favorites."

"Not until you eat all your dinner," Max said, staring down his nose at her like some gruff nanny. "I would offer you some wine, but Mrs. Putnam clearly indicated that you were to have nothing but the chilled cider."

"Blast! Was never a person so beset by people who have only her best interests at heart. Whatever happened to the willful orphan who could do exactly as she wanted," she muttered, wrinkling her nose in disgust.

"She is eating a picnic lunch on the banks of the Thames," Max responded, earning a sniff from his companion.

They ate between bursts of conversation, thoroughly enjoying the novelty of the alfresco repast. The sound of the water bubbling past was a fitting counterpoint to the singing of birds in the nearby trees. Despite the admonitions of her chaperon, Amity untied her bonnet and threw it down on the grass.

"You shall return with a nose all red and freck-led," Max warned.

"I know, but I hate always wearing a hat. It's wonderful to feel the sun on my hair." Amity lifted the weight of her hair from her neck and raised her arms to pile it atop her head. She looked up, notic-ing the arrested expression on her guardian's face. "Max?" she asked in question.

Max shook his head. "It's nothing, my dear." He dropped his eyes from the wood sprite who sat op-posite him. He was glad she had worn her hair down today. She had been wearing it bound up lately, and he had missed the ripple of curls that cascaded down her back. He could hardly tell her that for a moment, he had wanted to bury his hands in the fiery silk of her hair. It was hardly a guardianlike comment.

After lunch they put away the remains of the food and returned everything to the grinning Lewis, who was busily tucking into a lunch basket of his own. Then with her hat properly in place and her parasol over her shoulder, Amity took the arm Max ex-tended and they set off down the lane.

There was much to see along the banks of the river. Flowers abounded, growing wild for the most part, but in some places lovingly tended by the women in the nearby cottages. Occasionally they passed a villager, and Amity would stop and enter into conversation, her face piquant as she listened to the respectful answers to her myriad questions. Eventually Max would drag her away, complaining that he was being wholly neglected.

It was on their return that they spotted the boys. Max had been telling Amity about some of the an-

tics of his brother just prior to his being sent down
from Cambridge, when he noticed that her attention was no longer on the story.

Amity's eyes narrowed as she watched a group of
boys placing a squirming object in a small wooden
cask. She raised her voice in a shout, and the boys
turned startled faces in her direction. After a whispered conference, the biggest boy raised the cask
over his head and threw it into the water. Then
shouting wildly, the boys raced away from the river,
disappearing quickly from sight.

"Hurry, Max," Amity yelled and, picking up her
skirts, ran to the edge of the water.

"What is it?" Max said as he came up to her at
a more leisurely pace.

"It's a cat, I think." Her eyes scanned the surface
of the water, and with a shout she caught hold of
his arm, pointing at the wooden object bobbing a
short distance away. "They put it inside the cask."

"Well, I fear, my girl, there is nothing we can do
for it. If it's not drowned already, it soon will be."

Max's practical words did little to dampen her
need for action. She flung an exasperated glance in
his direction before dashing along the bank, following the progress of the cat-laden vessel. She closed
her parasol and extended it over the water, hoping
the cask would float nearer. The barrel remained
tantalizingly beyond reach, and her face took on an
anguished expression as the wooden cask sank
lower in the water. Max could not stand to see her
suffer over the fate of the cat, so he scanned the
area ahead until he thought he had found a logical
spot to execute a rescue.

"Come along, Amity," he said, grabbing her hand

and pulling her along in his wake. "There's a place farther down where the river bends. We'll try for it there."

Her face full of gratitude was reward enough for his insanity and lent wings to their feet as they raced along beside the river. Reaching the spot where the bank jutted out over the water, Max ripped off his jacket and grabbed a handful of tall bushes for purchase.

"Now open your parasol and give me your hand. No, the other one so you can see what you're doing. Brace your feet against mine, and I shall lower you over the water."

Amity followed his directions, grinning as the hem of her skirts dipped dangerously close to the water. She kept her eyes fastened to the bobbing cask and was overjoyed to see that if it maintained its position, she should be able to scoop it up with the opened parasol as it passed.

"Get ready," Max shouted in encouragement.

He extended his arm as the barrel approached and cheered as she reached out to capture the prize. Just as the cask floated into the parasol, the bank gave way underneath his feet, and he lost his grip on the bushes holding him onto dry ground. Max's shout and Amity's squeal were lost in the sound of the enormous splash as both of them hit the water.

For a moment Amity was blinded, but realized it was only the soggy brim of her hat, and with her hands she pushed it away from her eyes. She tried not to panic and struggled to keep her head out of the water. Her skirts hampered her movements, but as she thrashed about, she discovered that the water was only about a foot deep. She let her body sink until she was sitting on the bottom, then turned to the sound of cursing coming from behind her.

Max lay on his stomach in about six inches of water, swearing steadily under his breath. He raised his head, and he glared malevolently at the barrel still imprisoned in the cheerful red parasol, which had grounded on the edge of the bank.

"Damnable creature!" he snarled.

"It wasn't the cat's fault!" Amity shouted in defense of the poor animal. "You were the one who let go of the bushes."

"I did not let go," he answered through gritted teeth. "You were too heavy to hold. You must have gained four stone since your arrival in London."

"What a horrid thing to say, you loathsome man." In her fury Amity slapped the water with her clenched fish, sending a wave splashing into Max's face.

Amid sputtering and coughing, he pushed himself to his hands and knees and launched himself at the girl, catching her up in a bear hug. They rolled over and over in the shallow water like children at play. Amid lighthearted shrieks, they splashed each other until they were both breathless from laughing. Finally, in exhaustion, Amity lay gasping in the circle of Max's arms.

"Oh, my adorable Amity," he whispered, staring down into her face.

She had never looked more beautiful, he thought, caught in a spell of wonder. Water ran like tears down her flushed cheeks, and her eyes sparkled with mischief. Without conscious thought he lowered his head, his lips softly covering hers in the tenderest of kisses. He felt her body shiver at the contact, but then she sighed in contentment.

Amity enjoyed the feel of Max's lips against her own, reminded again of Bancroft's sweet salutation. Then suddenly his mouth shifted, and there was a new urgency to his embrace. His lips sucked at hers, demanding a response, and they parted beneath the pressure. The touch of his tongue jolted her with a sweep of sensations that threatened to engulf her. Her heart pounded in her ears, and she tightened her grasp around his shoulders as her stomach fluttered with the sensation of falling. Her body rippled with waves of excitement, and she moaned at the sheer ecstasy of the moment.

The sound echoed mournfully across the water, and Amity was stunned into a realization of the impropriety of her actions. She pushed against Max's chest, and his arms released her immediately as if he, too, were aware of his ungentlemanly behavior.

"Forgive me, Amity," he whispered hoarsely.

Amity refused to think about the emotions Max's kiss had raised in her breast. She knew she had behaved wantonly in accepting his embrace and now only wanted to break the awkwardness that would ensue if she gave in to any missish sentiments.

"Please, Max," she reached out to place her hand on his chest. "It was the joy of the moment. A kiss between friends. We are friends, are we not?" she asked brightly.

"We are indeed, my dear." Max felt doubly guilty under the lightness of her tone. It was apparent she wished to restore their relationship, and he could

only applaud her actions. There would be time later
to analyze what had occurred, but for now he must
put the episode behind him. He lifted her hand from
his chest and kissed it with clownish enthusiasm,
earning a shaky giggle for his playacting. "Come,
my bedraggled mermaid. It is time to seek dry
land."

He struggled to his feet, then extended a hand to
help her out of the water. They scrambled up and
stood dripping on the bank. Max looked her up and
down and slowly amusement erased his feeling of
embarrassment. He began to chuckle at the outraged dignity on Amity's face and threw his head
back in great yelps of laughter. Amity looked down
at herself and groaned in dismay. The once white
dress was now stained with mud, and there were
places where the red ribbons had bled onto the
white material. Ignoring his amusement, she pulled
the parasol out of the water and dumped the barrel
on dry land. Then she turned to face Max and spun
the parasol, enveloping him in a fine mist of spray.

"Cheeky wench," Max muttered, wiping his face
with his sleeve.

"You can hardly laugh at me, you gudgeon, looking as you do."

Ruefully he eyed his cream-colored trousers,
which were soaked and streaked with mud. The lace
at his wrists drooped pathetically over his hands,
and his once crisp cravat snaked down his chest
like something long dead. Imagining Wilberforce's
horrified expression, he began to chuckle anew. He
squished across the grass to retrieve his jacket and
placed it over Amity's shoulders with a flourish.

"Your cloak, madam," he said, making her an elegant leg.

She raised her dripping skirts and bobbed a curtsy. Then she flipped a strand of hair over her shoulder and repositioned her hat on her head. The brim flopped maddeningly in front of her eyes, and hearing Max's choked laughter, she giggled and removed the offending object.

"Just wait until Lady Grassmere sees what I've done to my new bonnet," she mumbled.

"I fear Cousin Hester will go into spasms if she sees either of us," he said, rolling his eyes and wiggling his eyebrows. "And all for the sake of a cat."

"The cat!" Amity shrieked, dropping down beside the cask in order to free the poor animal. Max knelt beside her, prying open the top. The cat sprang out of the barrel in a burst of hissing and clawing.

In the bright afternoon sunlight the cat was far from a prepossessing sight. She was fat with a face that looked entirely too sly to be pleasing. Her ginger-colored fur was wet and stood up in spiky patches along her back. Her gray-brown eyes narrowed as she lunged out at the person nearest to her.

"Steady on, you beast," Max snapped as the infuriated ball of sodden fur swiped at him.

Amity chuckled at his insulted tone. "She does not know you are truly a hero," she apologized.

"Ungrateful hussy," he sneered. "I shall have none of her either."

He pushed himself to his feet and helped Amity up, pulling her hand through his arm. He started back down the lane, trying to ignore the squelching sounds his boots made at every step. "We shall pretend that nothing is amiss, and then we should be able to pass quite unnoticed."

Amity stared at him openmouthed, but as he peered at her out of the corner of his eye, she once more started to giggle. "For a moment there, I almost believed you."

"Ah, well, I suspect we are in for a dreadful scold, so I see little to be gained by worrying about it."

They both agreed and continued on their way, chatting amiably until they arrived at the carriage, and Lewis gaped in astonishment.

"So much for your theory," Amity said cheekily. "You can explain while I get the cat. Come here, Ginger."

"Don't tell me that miserable excuse for a feline has followed us," Max burst out in exasperation. He glared down at the matted fur of the ginger cat, hardening his heart at the woebegone look on its feline face. "I much preferred it in the barrel."

Amity dropped to the ground, scooping up the bedraggled cat and cuddling it against her damp bosom. "Oh, Max, I suspect that it's just hungry and lonely."

"Don't say it," he warned. "I don't care if it needs a good home." Then at the appeal in her eyes, he threw up his hands in resignation. "All right, but only if you promise to keep it in the storeroom."

"It'll chase the chickens!" she argued.

"What chickens?" he shouted. "Devil take it, you baggage! Just keep it out of my sight." For a moment his eyes narrowed as he caught the glint of smugness on the cat's face, but he shook his head at his own fancy.

Lewis, his eyes shifting back and forth between

the brangling couple, was hard pressed to keep from laughing. Suspecting his master's humor might be strained to the edge, he held his tongue all the way back to town.

Max took a circuitous route through the city, avoiding the better sections where they were most likely to run into someone they knew. Instead of pulling up in front of the town house, he brought the curricle into the mews. He ignored the stares of the servants as he fastidiously removed the cat from Amity's lap and presented it to Lewis with orders to see to its care. Then with unhurried formality, he handed Amity to the ground, leading her quickly through the garden to the kitchen entrance. There, unfortunately, their luck ran out.

"Miss Amity!" Betta gasped, knocking over her tea in her haste to rise.

"Your lordship!" Wilberforce chimed in, followed by a chorus of excited voices.

Drawing on centuries of arrogant ancestors, Max stared around the room until the hubbub subsided. Then in stentorian tones he snapped out a series of orders that left the inhabitants of the room scurrying to comply. Finished, he extended his hand to Amity and ushered her up the backstairs with great dignity. It was only in the upstairs hall that his composure cracked, and he let out a great sigh of relief.

"Run along now, before Cousin Hester sees you, or she will fall down in fits."

"I hope Wilberforce does not scold you too badly," she whispered. Then standing on tiptoe she kissed his cheek. "Thank you for the memorable day, Max."

She scampered down the hall before Max could even lift his hand to touch the spot where her lips had touched his cheek. His face unreadable, he turned in the opposite direction toward his room.

Knowing that Betta would be along momentarily, Amity began to strip off her wet clothing. She wrapped herself in a dressing gown and curled up in a chair until her abigail called to tell her the bath was ready. She sighed in pure happiness as she sank into the hot water. While she bathed, she told Betta about rescuing the cat, avoiding the questioning look in her friend's eye at the end of the recital.

By the time she was finished drying her hair, shadows had lengthened in the room, and Betta hurried to light the candles. When Amity requested a tray in her room, explaining that she planned to go to bed early after the excitement of the day, the abigail looked surprised, but made no comment. She merely gathered the wet clothing in a bundle and slipped out the door.

Alone at last, Amity piled the pillows against the headboard and climbed into bed. She pulled the comforter up to her chin as a large tear rolled out of the corner of her eye and slipped silently down her cheek. She had held herself under such tight control that now she gave in to the pain that engulfed her. As if the floodgates had been opened, more and more tears fell, until the edge of the comforter was fairly soaked. Amity cried silently for several minutes, then on a shuddering sigh, she began to gain control of the situation.

The source of her anguish was the certain knowledge that she was in love with Max. She had realized it the moment his lips touched hers with the shattering kiss in the river. She had known it then, at the same time that she accepted the fact that he did not love her. He had kissed her out of joy, in the happiness of the moment. If he thought of her at all, it was with slight annoyance that she had intruded on his life.

In their many talks, she had come to understand what Max wanted in a wife. He wanted a woman who could act the lady, conduct herself with dignity, and not intrude on his affairs. For a moment she considered the possibility that he might one day see her as a perfect lady, but her mouth curled up in an ironic smile as she realized the impossibility of her ever playing that role. She was too honest to counterfeit virtues she did not have, and the qualities she possessed did not include the ones Max considered of highest priority. He would never see her as anything but a scatterbrained, hurly-burly girl. For Max the perfect lady was Honoria Waterston.

In despair Amity wondered what she should do. In two days' time she would be betrothed to Bancroft Paige. She had thought that she would eventually learn to love Bancroft, but Max's kiss had shown her the emotional upheaval of real love. Since she did not love him, was it fair to marry Bancroft? In a moment of perception, she realized that he did not require her love. He wanted a wife and she would be a good one. She had already given her heart, but she could strive to be the helpmate that he needed. She would be kind to his sister, bear his children, and try to be a docile and loving wife. Her life would be fruitful and gratifying without the painful emotions engendered by love.

Amity curled up beneath the covers, turning her face into the pillow. She remembered the first time she had seen Max, and the pain she had felt at his rejection. She had survived then, and she would most probably survive now. Sleep came slowly, easing the ache in her heart.

Chapter Eleven

Aside from the occasional rustle of a paper, the low-voiced instructions to a servant, or the raspy clearing of a throat, the main salon of Max's club was silent. He had commandeered a deeply padded leather chair in a small alcove and was sunk in a trancelike concentration. Intruders on his refuge had quickly scurried away, put off by the black-browed scowl he sent their way. Jurvis kept his snifter of brandy well filled, taking particular pains to avoid any noise that might disturb him.

Since early evening Max had been ensconced in the chair, sipping brandy and staring out the window. The view was unpromising, merely the side of the building next door, but he appeared to find the blank wall a fascinating subject for perusal. From time to time his lips moved as if he were holding a serious colloquy with an invisible friend, then he would shake his head in negation and return to his examination of the building outside the window.

Lord Devereaux Havenhurst stood at the side of the room, watching the antics of his friend, and a slow smile broke the ascetic quality of his face.

When he had asked the faithful Jurvis if he had seen Lord Kampford, the servant had cautioned him that his friend seemed in an unusually somber frame of mind. It was interesting to find the unflappable, methodical Max looking totally unsettled. Dev arranged his features in a more serious mien and approached the alcove.

"Would you mind if I joined you, sir?"

Max was so deeply involved in his own thoughts that he did not immediately recognize Dev's voice. He emitted a low growling sound and glared up at the interloper, only to be met by a familiar pair of twinkling blue eyes.

"Dev, old man!" Max exclaimed. He leaped to his feet and grasped the extended hand, gripping it with an enthusiastic shake. "Pull up a chair. Can you stay for a while or are you on your way to an engagement?"

Dropping down in the chair at right angles to Max, Dev said, "I have the entire evening free. I am yours to command."

"Good show! I have no plans either so I will enjoy the company."

"Are you sure? When I asked to join you, I thought you might run me through," Dev said, cocking an eyebrow in question.

"My apologies. I have been sadly blue-deviled this evening, but now that you are here, I feel my spirits returning to a better humor." Max raised his glass just as Jurvis arrived with a snifter for Dev. They saluted each other, and Max took a sip of the heady liquor. "What brings you to town? I assumed you were happily moldering in the country, awaiting the heir to the Havenhurst fortune. Speaking of which, how is Jena?"

"As to your second question, my darling wife is blooming with health. She bewails the fact that in profile she appears to be carrying some misshapen behemoth, but quite frankly I have never seen her look more beautiful." Dev beamed in pride at his approaching fatherhood. "There are still three months to go before the appearance of the much awaited heir, and already my grandfather is demanding that we move to Waverly for the confinement."

"Will you go?" Max asked, amused as always by news of the feisty Duke of Waverly.

Dev pushed a hand through his white hair and grimaced. "I fear the old man will give me no peace unless we accede to his wishes. Jena dotes on the curmudgeon and has agreed, on the condition that we return in time for the foaling season."

"I wish you both well," Max said, his face serious. He raised his snifter. "To the health and happiness of your lady wife."

"To Jena!" Dev raised his glass, then took a long swallow before he continued. "Now, as to your first question, I am come to town to handle the transfer of some property. Nothing particularly involved, but it gave me a chance to stop for a visit and bring you up to date on the latest news from the country. I am chagrined to report that my wife has been most successful in her quest. Reggie is getting married."

"Devil you say! I never imagined our friend would take the plunge. Your Jena is definitely a matchmaker to be wary of. Do I know the girl?"

"Don't think so. Diane Farrington. Family's big

in hunting circles. Father's the Hunting Vicar of Frostiglade. She's young, only eighteen, and she's a neck-or-nothing rider. Quite surprising really, since she's a little bit of a blond thing with great cornflower eyes and a wispy voice. On the back of a horse, she's something ferocious."

Max's eyes wandered to the blank wall outside the window as he reviewed the many escapades in which he, Dev, Reggie, and the lumbering Dickon had been involved. Dev was married and now Reggie. The old days were gone.

"I'm glad for him, Dev. When you see him, be sure and convey my sincerest wishes," he said.

"He mentioned that he hoped you would come north for the wedding. After all, it seems only fitting for the four of us to have one more bacchanalian feast," Dev announced, grinning when Max nodded in agreement. "By the way, my friend, what of your own marital plans? When last we spoke you were heading for London with an antidote of a ward and a yearning to be leg-shackled."

For the first time in their conversation, the frown returned to Max's face. "In actual fact, old chum, the antidote ward turned out to be a butterfly of outstanding beauty. It seems I will have her off my hands quite soon. Tomorrow I believe she will be announcing her betrothal."

Dev noted the tightness of Max's mouth as he bit off the last words. There was definitely something wrong here, and he suspected it was the reason his friend had been so Friday-faced when he arrived. "Do not leave me in the dark. I wish to know all of the details of the beauteous, eh, Endurance, if my memory serves me."

Max laughed in remembrance. "I had quite forgotten. When she arrived, we agreed that Amity would be far more preferable. Although now that I think on it, as her guardian I have had a great deal to endure."

Slowly Max began to tell of all that had transpired since Amity came to intrude on his well-regulated bachelor existence. Dev noted how his friend's voice softened when he spoke of the girl, and how often Max laughed over her unusual antics. It was wholly apparent to Dev that he was deeply in love with his ward, but he was not sure if Max even realized that fact.

"What a delightfully enterprising wench," Dev said as the recital came to an end. "Jobs for soldiers. What a novel idea."

"I was sure you would appreciate that part of the story, since Jena was involved in a similar scheme. Except as I recall, she hired the most disreputable specimens it has ever been my good fortune to encounter."

"A lovably scurvy lot," Dev agreed, chuckling deeply before he continued. "And you say that despite all Amity's activities, you have managed to arrange a marriage?"

"Not arranged exactly. She had offers aplenty, which for various reasons I turned down as not being quite the thing. The last offer was from a very eligible party. Lord Bancroft Paige. Do you know him?"

"Blond curls and the face of a cupid?"

Max snorted in amusement. "That fairly well sums it up. Good family. Pots of money. She's a lucky girl."

These last words were said with a sneering tone, suggesting to Dev that perhaps there was still hope for Max. "Don't sound as though you half like the man."

Max's forehead wrinkled as he frowned. He leaned forward and lowered his voice. "Actually I have nothing against him, Dev. He's above reproach in many ways. There's never been a hint of scandal bandied about, and I suspect all things considered, he would make a reasonably good husband. I just do not feel he will be good for Amity."

"In what way?" Dev asked cautiously.

Max threw himself against the leather back of the chair. "In every way," he growled. "Without knowing Amity, it is difficult to explain what she is like. She's volatile and impetuous, inveterately curious and incredibly free-spirited. She needs a strong hand to keep her from running off on some half-baked scheme, without keeping the control so tight that it breaks her spirit, or she rebels. Beyond that, she needs someone who can enter into her activities with a sense of fun."

"The Bancroft Paige I remember does not possess many of those qualities," Dev remarked dryly. "Rather a lofty type if I recall correctly."

"He's dry as a bone, Dev. Doubt if the man has a lick of humor anywhere in his whole body. He will be appalled once he discovers the kind of girl she is. He will have no idea what a treasure he possesses, but will try to bend her into a mold of convention. She will not bend; she will break."

Max's words quite unsettled him, and there was a light of anguish that beamed from his eyes as he stared down into his drink. Dev was totally perplexed, not knowing what to do for the best. He hated seeing his friend so distraught, but he was loath to interfere. For the moment he thought it was best to change the subject since he needed further enlightenment to understand the full problem.

"And how goes your campaign to find the perfect fiancée?"

If anything, Max looked more disturbed by the question. "Devil take it, Dev! I thought I had my entire life under control. Now I wonder if I have sense enough to come in out of a rain."

"It would seem, old chum, that from the exasperation I see in your eyes, you have made an almighty hash of the whole project." Dev grinned at his friend's snort of disgust. "I told you once that men were not intended to understand women."

"To my shame I will admit that I scoffed at that statement." Once more Max leaned forward, his face set in an earnest expression. "I thought I really did understand what made the perfect wife. But in the last several months I find that what I want, and what I think I want, are not the same things."

"Perhaps they are, Max. There was a time in my life when I was convinced that marrying Jena was the worst of disasters. Eventually I began to realize that if I stopped fighting the inevitable, the greatest happiness would be mine. Love caught me unaware, but now I truly believe in its power."

Dev was silent for a moment as he gauged his friend's reaction. He knew that with Max's background, he had tried to create an oasis of order and method in his life. Love was irrational and as such would be difficult for Max to come to terms with. Listening objectively to his friend's description of

his dealings with Amity, Dev had sensed an under-
lying core of happiness that had been totally absent
before.

"What do you think you want?" Dev asked quietly.

"I thought I wanted Honoria Waterston. It is very
strange, however; lately I have begun to wonder if
in fact she is only a lady in appearance. For me a
lady should have goodness, honesty, humor, and
moral strength. Because Honoria looked the part of
the lady, I assumed she possessed all of these qualities, but in actual fact I suspect she has none. I
sensed she would conform to convention and never
give me a reason to worry about her conduct unless
I looked too closely at her activities. I think I was
delighted with the restfulness I felt in her presence,
a freedom of emotional involvement. Now I wonder
if I will not die of boredom with that sort of relationship."

"What do you really want, Max?"

"Damn it all, Dev. I want Amity!"

"Ah ha, my friend. At last you are honest with
me," he grinned across at his disgruntled friend.
"When you described Amity, I did not feel that her
actions were vulgar or tasteless."

"That is the confusing part of this whole thing.
She is the exact antithesis of my idea of a proper
lady, and yet in her I find all the qualities of a real
lady. The servants adore her, and you know how
starched-up my staff is. She is strong and fine and
good." Max sounded as though he had just listed
all her worst characteristics.

"Are you in love with her?"

"Yes, damn it! She makes me laugh," Max

snapped, glaring at Dev as if to dare him to sneer at such an illogical statement. "She came bursting into my well-ordered life and invaded all the rooms of my house like a horde of avenging Berbers. I grumbled and grumped, but discovered an ability to laugh that I have not had since I was a child. She's like sunshine, quicksilver, and I find the thought of losing her to some starched-up stick of a man quite unbearable."

"It would seem to me, Max, that you ought to make some push in her direction. The man of action I used to recall would hardly sit all evening at his club, swilling brandy and feeling sorry for himself." Dev's face took on a haughty expression, and he stared balefully at Max. "Have you mentioned your feelings to the girl?"

"Of course not, Dev! That would be highly improper since I am, as you recall, her guardian." Suddenly he shifted in his chair, and a flush invaded the whiteness of his face. Dev raised an eyebrow in question. "It was nothing," Max said hastily.

"Stubble it!"

"All right. All right. I kissed her, if you must know." Max raised a hand quickly in defense. "It happened when we fell in the water trying to rescue a cat. It meant nothing. It was the excitement of the moment, and it was forgotten immediately afterward. Naturally I apologized. Amity was slightly flustered, but she puffed it off as just a kiss between friends."

"And you bought that? Good Lord, Max. You really have got straw in your cockloft," Dev crowed. "So you will let your ward marry a totally unsuitable man while you do nothing to prevent it? Strange actions for a guardian. By the way, I find it hard to believe that the inventive Miss Amity you have described is in love with the unexciting Lord Bancroft Paige. Why is she marrying him?"

"Because I told her to," Max growled. "As her guardian it is my duty to advise her. She trusts me implicitly. I told her I thought it would be an excellent arrangement." Dev merely stared down his nose in condemnation of such stupidity. "What could I say? I was not aware of my feelings at the time. Besides, she does not think of me in any way other than as her guardian."

"Are you sure? Did she seem horrified when you kissed her?"

"Well, no. On the contrary, she appeared to quite enjoy the incident," Max said, a momentary glimmer of hope in his eyes. Then he shook his head in rejection. "She has not had much acquaintance with lovemaking, so I expect it was the novelty of the experience."

"Believe me, Max, if she did not have some feeling for you, she would have reacted with either horror or affront."

"Do you think so?"

There was a look of such expectation on Max's face that Dev nearly burst into laughter. "At least give the girl a chance. Besides, it matters not whether she can love you. As her guardian you cannot sit back and let her betroth herself to that stiff-necked Paige. You cannot ignore the situation."

"You're absolutely right, Dev," Max said with conviction, but immediately after his face took on an anguished look. "She told me once that she wanted to get married in order to have a baby, if you can believe that kind of nonsensical reasoning. She understands little about love because she has had so little in her life. Besides, she is convinced that I am about to offer for Honoria. I have given her no reason to expect otherwise, so I am not sure she will believe that I have had an abrupt change of mind. Worse than that, she has already accepted Bancroft. Even if I tell her I do not think he is the right man for her, she will still feel honor-bound to defend his suit. I understand her well enough to know she will never cry off and risk hurting Paige, despite the fact that he will make her most unhappy."

"In that case you will just have to convince Paige that she would make a very poor wife," Dev concluded.

"That's just what I'm trying to tell you. She will make a wonderful wife. Only a dolt and a dunderhead would not be able to see that!" When Max looked up, he noted the gleam of roguery in Dev's eyes, and he blinked in sudden awareness. Slowly his mouth pulled wide in a devilish grin. "I say, old bean, are you suggesting that Lord Bancroft Paige might be a dolt and a dunderhead?"

Dev spread his hands in a gesture of innocence, and his blue eyes were guileless as he returned Max's glance. A deep chuckle rumbled up from Max's chest, and he raised his snifter in a final toast.

"To Paige."

"Hear! Hear!" responded Dev.

For Max it was like a return to the old days, and he wished Reggie and Dickon were here to join

forces. He moved his chair closer to Dev's, and they
began to consider possible strategies.

"Oh Betta, I shall shrivel up under Ophelia's disapproving eye," Amity wailed. "Whatever will I do
if Bancroft's sister cannot like me?"

"If you don't hold still, she will take one look at
your hair and run screaming from the room," the
harassed abigail said as she tried to anchor a hairpin in her mistress's coiffure. Her plain face was
set in disapproval since she was not particularly
partial to Lord Bancroft Paige. She had had other
ideas as to who Miss Amity should marry.

"I'm sorry, Betta," Amity apologized, smiling at
her friend in the mirror above the vanity. "I am
just so nervous."

"You have no reason to be nervous, Miss Amity.
If she can't take you the way you are, then there's
no point in worrying. Better you should wonder
what is wrong with her if she cannot like you."

Amity giggled. "I wish I had your good sense, my
girl. I always feel better for telling you my troubles."

Betta noticed the dark circles under her mistress's eyes and suspected that she had not shared
all her troubles. She was very curious as to what
had transpired on the picnic when she had returned
all wet and disheveled, but Miss Amity had been
unusually quiet ever since. More curious still, Lord
Maxwell Kampford had been decidedly absent since
that day, almost as if he were avoiding his own
town house. Betta jammed the last hairpin into
place none too gently and stood back eyeing her
charge.

"How do I look?" Amity asked, rising and turning slowly before her abigail.

Despite a slightly subdued air about her, Amity looked magnificent. Her gown was a heavy moss green silk, which softened the red tones of her hair and brought out the gold highlights. There was a wide band of cream-colored lace at the high neck, repeated again at the wrists and along the edge of the hem. The lines of the dress were exceedingly simple. The bodice was made up of flat pleats to just beneath her breasts, then the skirt fell to the floor in a shimmer of silk. She wore no jewelry, except a string of pearls that Betta knew had been given to her by Lord Kampford. Her hair was dressed in a Psyche knot, and its simplicity accentuated the exotic beauty of her crystal blue eyes.

"I expect you'll do," Betta said dryly. "Especially if Lord Paige is expecting a princess."

"What a good friend you are," Amity said, hugging her in a burst of enthusiasm. Then her eyes flew to the clock and she gasped. "They will be here any minute. Oh, I wonder if Max and Lady Grassmere are ready."

"I almost forgot," Betta said, reaching into the pocket of her apron and extracting a note. "Lord Kampford said I was to give this to you when you were ready."

Amity snatched the paper and with shaking fingers ripped open the note. A smile was forming on her face at the thought of her guardian's kindness until she read the words of the note: "Just remember to take a deep breath every quarter hour and then everything is sure to go well." Oh, why did he have to remind her of her habit of knocking things over in her nervousness. Just the mere mention of it gave her a queer feeling in the pit of her stomach, and she crumpled the note in annoyance.

"Blast!" she swore.

"Miss Amity!"

"Oh, I know! I shan't say it again." Amity dropped the paper on the vanity and called to Muffin, who was as usual ensconced on the chaise longue. "Come on, old boy. It's time to put in an appearance."

The dog slid to the floor unenthusiastically and followed his mistress to the door. She dug her fingers into the fur at his neck, grateful for the comforting contact with the animal. Sedately they walked through the hallway and down the stairs to the salon. Lady Grassmere and Max were already present.

Max rose to his feet, and Amity flushed at the gleam of appreciation in his eyes. He came forward and with a chivalrous gesture raised her hand to his lips. A shiver ran down her spine as his lips touched her skin, and she strove to control the rush of feeling that pounded along her nerve endings.

"My dear, there is little question that neither Bancroft nor Ophelia will find anything to criticize," Max said, his deep voice full of praise. "You are truly exquisite."

"Thank you, Max," Amity said stiffly. She snatched her hand away, but still felt the touch of his lips as if they had marked her forever. Unable to meet his eyes, she turned quickly to her chaperon. "How elegant you look, Lady Grassmere. Is that a new dress?"

"Why, how clever of you to notice, child," Hester

said, flushing as she straightened the gray folds of her dress. "I thought this occasion deserved something special."

At this point the conversation came to a halt, and Amity sat down abruptly on the silver and white striped settee with Muffin sprawled at her feet. She fidgeted with her reticule and prayed that Bancroft and his sister would arrive soon. Her nerves felt totally overset; she had a sudden urge to giggle, but dug her nails into the palm of her hand until she was able to overcome such an idiotic notion. When she looked up, Max was leaning against the back of the high-backed chair next to the settee, his face quite expressionless.

Amity stared at him, wanting to imprint the memory of him on her mind. He looked well in black, she decided, for it brought out the unusual green in his eyes and made the chestnut color of his hair seem richer. His cravat, obviously the work of the indefatigable Wilberforce, was tied far more ornately than usual. Oh, how handsome he is, she thought as her eyes studied him.

A small furrow creased her forehead as she looked more closely at her guardian. Today there was something different about him. Although he appeared relaxed there was an air of tension to his body, almost as if he was prepared to do battle. Suddenly he glanced across at her, and there was a blaze of intensity in his green eyes that she could not read. Then his mouth flashed in a wide grin that transformed his face, and there was such a feeling of happiness apparent in his smile that Amity was quite taken aback. She was saddened that he was so pleased to have her finally off his hands.

When Putnam announced Lord and Lady Paige, she had to force a smile of welcome to her trembling lips.

While they were greeting Max and Lady Grassmere, Amity had a chance to study Ophelia. Her first impression was not promising. The thirty-year-old spinster was wearing a gown of dun-colored sarcenet devoid of frivolous trim or ornamentation. A small round cap of worked muslin covered her hair, except for a thin braid of mousy hair that was bound in a tight bun at the nape of her neck. Ophelia might have been considered a neat and trim woman, but for the look of disapproval she wore like a banner on her face. Her mouth was pinched into a thin discontented line and her dark eyes held little softness.

Amity trembled as Max led Ophelia over to the settee and waited as he seated her, asking solicitously if she were quite comfortable.

"My comfort is of little importance to me," Ophelia said, her voice a heavy monotone.

"My sister is known for her ability to withstand great physical inconvenience," Bancroft stated proudly. "She has a toughness of spirit that is much to be admired. She will be an excellent example for my future wife," he finished, reddening slightly as he stared pointedly at Amity.

"As Brother says, I would hope to be not only an example, but a guide for the young lady he favors with his attentions," Ophelia in her turn pointedly avoided looking at Amity, her eyes fixed balefully on Bancroft. "We live a simple life, free from the debilitating corruption of luxuries. A lady must learn to live with discomfort."

"A lowering thought, Lady Paige," Max said, his expression very serious although Amity caught a twinkle in the green depths. He seated himself in the high-backed chair, cocking his head as if listening. "Ah, here is our tea."

The doors to the salon were thrown open, and Putnam entered, followed by several footmen bearing trays. Max indicated that the tea tray should be set before Amity, whose hands were clenched nervously in her lap. She raised agonized eyes to her guardian, and he raised his pocket watch, taking a deep breath to remind her of his note. She ground her teeth at his conspicuous prompting, knowing only too well that his kindness in reminding her made her only too aware of her penchant for knocking things over. Blast Max's good intentions! she muttered under her breath. Steeling herself, she reached for the first cup.

"How would you like your tea, Lady Paige?" Amity asked, hoping the woman did not hear the distinct rattle of the china.

"Plain," was the uncompromising answer. "I have not always been able to convince Brother"—she nodded to Bancroft, who shifted self-consciously under her censuring gaze—"to give up his sweets. I find that most of the younger set cosset themselves with all sorts of confectioneries that do little to improve the health or teach them abstemious ways."

"How true, Lady Paige," Max said. He leaned against the cushioned arm, his hand tapping the cover of the wicker sewing basket beside the chair. "I have warned my ward that a diet of sticky buns will do little to enhance her figure. But then it is an innocent enough vice."

Amity stared daggers at Max, but managed a smile as Ophelia, mouth pinched in disapproval, turned to her. "Lord Kampford will have his little joke. I particularly abhor sticky buns," she said, drawing in a deep breath before she filled Lady Paige's cup. She passed it without incident, wanting to wipe her perspiring hands on her skirts before attempting another.

"Will you be leaving town soon, Lady Paige?" Max asked, his eyebrows raised in interested question. "Now that the summer heat has arrived, it appears to be quite uncomfortable."

"Brother and I will be going to Bath," she said, her words sparing, as if she begrudged the use of each one. "As a child, Bancroft was a puny thing, but each year I have seen to it that he takes the waters. As you can see, he has benefited from such an efficacious cure."

"Ophelia has been lucky to find rooms near the Crescent," Bancroft said, smiling fondly at his sister. "She is able to walk to the Pump Room each day for her morning glass. Since I am never quite sure how long I will be staying, I have been putting up at the inn. But Sister prefers to stay as long as the company is interesting."

"I was never a great believer in drinking medicinal waters," Max said, earning a look of condemnation from Ophelia. "Believe me, Lady Paige, you are far braver than I. I was in Bath for a week a year ago and availed myself of the much vaunted cure. One taste and I poured out my glass into the nearest potted plant. By the end of my stay, the plant looked decidedly peaked and was beginning to turn brown."

Bancroft chuckled at the joke as he leaned over the tea table, accepting the cup for Lady Grassmere and carrying it across to the chaperon, who was busy with the needlework in her lap.

"You look exceptionally well, Amity," he said when he returned to her side.

Before Amity could thank him for the compliment, Max leaned over to Ophelia and whispered in a voice that was quite audible to all, "You will be quite pleased that Amity has such a nicety of taste. She never stints on her wardrobe, but the extravagant prices are well worth it for the *savoir faire* of her ensembles."

One look at Ophelia's face sent Amity's heart plummeting to her satin slippers. The woman did not exactly sniff, but it was apparent she could not applaud either extravagance or *savoir faire*. A tremor invaded her arm as she extended Bancroft's cup. She was saved from disaster when he removed it from her hand, and she heaved a sigh of relief.

"I must agree that your ward is always very tastefully dressed," Bancroft said quickly into the heavy silence of the room.

For a moment Amity had an overpowering urge to stick her tongue out at Max. He was oblivious to her beau's ready defense, seemingly concentrating his attention on the ceiling, while his hand played with the lid of the wicker basket beside his chair. She could not understand what he was about. His conversation thus far had been both outrageous and provocative. He must be aware that his comments were not easing an already tense situation.

Amity's fingers felt wooden as she poured her own tea and raised the cup to her lips. She took a sip, hoping the soothing brew would calm her rattled nerves. Wanting to signal Max her distress, she raised her eyes to glare across at him, but she was caught by the sight of the wicker basket, which seemed to be moving of its own volition. It was only when the top inched upward and a ginger-colored paw snaked over the rim that Amity dropped her cup.

Chapter Twelve

The teacup dropped from Amity's nerveless fingers, hitting once against the edge of the table before it toppled to the carpet. She opened her mouth to call a warning as the top of the wicker basket opened farther, but the words froze on her tongue. In slow motion the top raised and slid sideways onto the floor. With a loud hiss and a scrabbling of claws on the reedy sides, the ginger cat exploded from its wicker prison. She sprang into the air and with balletic grace landed in the very center of the tea table between the tea service and the pastries.

For a moment nobody moved, so transfixed were they by the unexpected apparition. Ginger swung her head, eyeing the tarts topped with cream. The tip of her rough tongue showed between her teeth, and she lowered her head toward the plate. The slight movement broke the spell. Max rose to his feet at the same time that Amity made a desperate lunge for the animal, knocking the pitcher of cream over on the tray. The clattering sound upset the cat, and she sprang from the table, clearing the teapot by inches and landing neatly in Ophelia's lap.

"Oh! Oh!" Ophelia shrieked, making frantic flailing motions at the animal. "Get this beast away from me!"

At the sudden commotion the recumbent Muffin raised his shaggy head. The sight of the bristling cat started an ominous, growling rumble deep in his throat, and he lumbered to his feet. When the dog attempted to bound into the fray, Amity threw her arms around his neck, holding him by sheer strength against her legs.

"Oh help!" Ophelia cried, her spine pressed to the back of the settee and her face set in a grimace of loathing.

"Allow me, Lady Paige," Max said, his voice softly coaxing as he reached for the ginger cat. "Naughty puss. Not you, Lady Paige. I was referring to the cat."

At Max's words Amity felt a bubble of hysteria rising to her throat and buried her face in Muffin's coat. As if things weren't bad enough already, the dog decided he would enter the melee, if not physically at least verbally, and let loose with a chorus of deep barks. Amity patted his back, trying to calm him.

Looking around the room, she was surprised to see that Max was the only one attempting to help. He was trying to pry the cat's claws from the fabric of Ophelia's dress. Bancroft, who might have made some push to be of assistance, stood helplessly beside the settee as if he had been turned to stone. Lady Grassmere had dropped her needlework in her lap and was watching the whole proceedings with the same interest she might have given to a stage play.

"Ah, that's got it," Max said as he released the last claw from Ophelia's skirt. As he picked up the cat, Muffin subsided, dropping once more to the floor where he emitted low growling noises to show his disapproval. "Here, Putnam. Remove Ginger to some other place, if you please."

He handed the cat to the red-faced butler, who had come running at the sound of the uproar. Holding the cat warily between his gloved hands, Putnam extended his arms straight from the shoulder and sedately retreated into the hall.

"There. I think that will be the end of that. My heartfelt apologies," Max said as he turned back to the room. "I can't imagine how that dreadful animal managed to get into the basket. No harm done. Allow me, my dear," he said leaning over to wipe the spilled cream from the silver tray.

Amity snatched the white handkerchief from her guardian's hand, her eyes narrowed in speculation. Turning quickly to Lady Paige, she blotted a few spots on the woman's dress. Ophelia was breathing with great gasps, and Amity wondered if she would be wise to offer her smelling salts. Aside from the heavy breathing, the tense silence in the room was almost palpable, but she was too embarrassed to think of anything to say that might mitigate the disaster.

"A cat! Such a sly, nasty creature. Can't abide them. It is inconceivable why anyone would permit animals to run tame in one's house," Ophelia snapped. "In the country there is some excuse for their presence, but in town their existence is beneath notice."

"Again I apologize, Lady Paige," Max said, hov-

ering over the distraught woman. "That you should
have been so discomposed by the cat, I find quite
unforgivable. Amity and I rescued her several days
ago from a watery grave in the Thames. My ward
has such compassion for the plight of animals in
distress. You would barely recognize that feisty
creature for the sodden feline we brought home. It
must gladden your heart to see it so restored to
health."

"I find its return to health no cause for celebra-
tion. Neither Bancroft nor I approve of house pets,"
Ophelia said dampeningly. "Isn't that right,
Brother?"

"Sister feels—that is, I feel," he said, looking
somewhat harried as he brushed the golden curls
away from his forehead, "that animals breed all
sorts of diseases and by and large are quite filthy.
I was never permitted to have a pet in the house
and once the reasoning was explained to me, I con-
curred with the decision wholeheartedly."

Muffin made a snuffling sound in his sleep, and
Amity leaned over to gently stroke his fur. Frowning, she stared down at the friend of her childhood,
wondering how she could have survived her lonely
years without his presence. It was readily apparent
that if she wished to marry Bancroft, she would be
forced to give up the companionship of her dog.
Slowly the lines in her forehead smoothed out, and
when she raised her head, her face was serene. She
folded her hands gracefully in her lap as the silence
lengthened around her.

"My dog is neither filthy nor a carrier of any dis-
ease. I have always kept him in the house near to

me," she said quietly. She stared up at Bancroft, her words clearly issuing a challenge.

He cleared his throat, his glance shifting quickly to his sister, who sat like some carved image of the god of wrath. He studied her mouth, pinched in condemnation, and her eyes, dark with purpose, then his eyes swung back to Amity, and there was a deep sadness within their depths. "I am sure he is a noble animal, my dear, but his place is clearly not in the house. I am very sorry."

No one moved in the room, and in the quiet his words took on a more doleful significance. Amity's blue eyes glittered brightly as she studied the man who had asked for her hand. Then with a brisk nod of her head, she spoke.

"I am very sorry, too," she said. Straightening her shoulders, she turned to Ophelia and held out her hand in a graceful gesture. "Thank you so much for coming today, Lady Paige. It was a pleasure getting to know you better. I know you will have other calls to make, so we shall not keep you. Perhaps we shall run into each other at another time."

Ophelia blinked her eyes several times in surprise as Amity helped her to her feet. They faced each other, and their eyes acknowledged what neither of them wished to put into words. A glimmer of satisfaction flitted across the older woman's face, quickly replaced by her usual disapproving frown. She reached out possessively for her brother's arm and graciously said her good-days. With the clearly bewildered Bancroft in tow, Ophelia sailed into the hall.

The salon doors closed, and Amity dropped once more onto the settee, contemplating the calamitous

events of the tea party. She could not believe that
so much had gone wrong. Even before Ginger made
her unexpected appearance, it was apparent that
Ophelia was hardly thrilled by her brother's choice
of a bride. And Max's behavior had done nothing
but exacerbate an already difficult situation. She
raised her eyes to her guardian, who was leaning
against the mantelpiece. He shuttered his eyes
quickly, but not before she surprised a look of satisfaction within the green depths.

"Well," Hester said. "This has been a most interesting affair."

Unused to Lady Grassmere offering any comment,
both Amity and Max were surprised at the woman's statement. Normally the little chaperon sat in
the room but rarely ventured an opinion, so that
now they both stared at attention as if waiting for
an oracle to offer some enlightening prediction.

"A very tiresome woman, Ophelia Paige," Hester
continued. "I do find her presence quite overpowering. Even as a child, she was a great trial to her
mother. It is no wonder she has never married."

"I didn't realize you did not care for Ophelia,"
Amity said.

"She's always been a bit high in the instep for
my taste. Your sharp tongue would have been quite
wasted on Bancroft, my dear," Hester said, smiling
across at Amity. "Like his sister, he has little humor."

"You don't mind that I will not be marrying Bancroft?" Amity asked in surprise.

"Quite to the contrary. He was not the person I
had in mind at all," Hester said. "I was only surprised that the situation had gotten so far out of

hand. It seemed for a time that I might have to speak to your guardian. Thankfully this extreme measure was not necessary."

Much to Amity's bewilderment, Max threw back his head in a great shout of laughter. His green eyes sparkled mischievously as he traded intelligence with the old woman in gray.

Lady Grassmere smiled at the handsome man. He had always been her favorite. Carefully she folded her needlework. "You always were an inventive lad, Maxwell. My concern was that you left it so long. I was not positive you would come to your senses before it was too late."

"I was not as perceptive as you, Cousin Hester," Max said as he rose. He crossed the carpet and helped the little woman out of her chair. Much to her surprise and obvious gratification, he leaned down and kissed her wrinkled cheek. "Perhaps you would care to lie down while I talk to Amity. In fact, I would not be surprised if Muffin is in need of a rest after such a fatiguing assault on our ears." By main force he managed to get the sleepy dog to his feet and practically carried him out of the room. Panting from the exertion, he turned to Hester. "Perhaps we might all gather later for a celebratory dinner," he said as he eased the chaperon and Muffin toward the doors.

"A splendid idea, dear boy," Hester said, eyes sparkling as she nudged the reluctant dog into the hall.

As the doors closed behind Cousin Hester and Muffin, the smile faded from Max's face, and he turned to stare at Amity, who was looking decidedly stunned by the proceedings. He shifted uneasily on the carpet, his hands behind his back, as he debated how best to broach the subject. He found no difficulty in discussing the aborted betrothal, but he had no idea if it was too soon to mention his own feelings.

Amity was totally mystified by the conversation between Lady Grassmere and her guardian. As she peeked at Max from behind lowered lashes, she acknowledged his nervousness, but also detected an expression of mischievous satisfaction. Her eyes narrowed as she thought back over the events of the afternoon. She blinked in surprise at her sudden suspicions.

"Why did you do it?" Amity blurted out into the silence.

"Do what?" Max's face was expressionless, his eyes guarded.

"Why did you sabotage the tea party? You sent me that note knowing full well that I would be overcome with nervousness at the mere thought of knocking something over," she accused. "Then you made all those provoking comments about sticky buns and my extravagance. And finally, you knew the cat was in the sewing basket. Did you put her in there?"

"Well yes," he admitted and waved his hand dismissively. "But it was just an experiment."

"A what?"

"An experiment," he repeated slowly as if speaking to a child. "I wasn't sure that you knew enough about Paige to make the best decision. I thought this might help you see a little clearer the kind of man you would be marrying."

"I thought you wanted me to marry Bancroft."

"I did, for a while. But the more I thought about it the less the idea appealed to me. On the one hand, he is well fixed financially and of course, has a perfectly blameless reputation. On the other, he has little humor, is decidedly stuffy, and has an impossible sister. After giving the situation a great deal of consideration, I decided that you would not suit."

"I see," Amity said, although she did not understand at all. She stared across at Max, surprised at the way he shifted uneasily beneath her glare. He seemed extremely ill at ease, a far cry from his usual composure and poise. "Why didn't you tell me you had decided that I shouldn't marry Bancroft?"

"I wasn't sure you would believe me," Max said, cautiously moving a step closer to the settee. "Besides, I wanted you to see for yourself exactly what kind of a situation you would be letting yourself in for if you accepted his suit. His sister runs that entire household, Bancroft included, and you would have found yourself caught between the two of them."

"I was already aware of that," she said quietly.

"And you would have married him anyway," Max snapped in exasperation.

"Yes." Amity's eyes fell under the angry green gaze of her guardian.

"That's just what I thought. But why were you willing to marry him, knowing what kind of existence you would lead?" Max's voice took on a wondering tone.

"I told you once that I wanted to have a family."

"Fine family Bancroft would have given you. Ophelia would probably take over the care of any children you might have. I am sure Sister would not have approved of your methods of raising them. Brother would naturally side with her, as the great arbiter of the Paige family traditions. And then where would you be, my girl?" He moved several steps closer and waited for Amity's response.

"I never thought of that," she said. She raised her head and there was a look of sadness written on her face. "Then it all would have been for nothing."

Amity's words made Max's heart lurch in his chest. He wanted to reach out and hold her, soothing away the misery that was so evident. The blue of her eyes was sadly dimmed, almost lifeless, and it hurt him to see her so affected. He knew he mustn't rush his fences, but suddenly he felt hope and sat down beside her on the settee. He reached out and patted her hands, easing one into his own warm palm. He stared down at her fingers, quite bewitched by the softness of her skin.

"I must admit to a slight curiosity. You do not appear to be particularly devastated by Bancroft's unwillingness to battle his sister for your favors," he said.

"I must confess, Max, that even before today I had some slight reservation as to how well we would deal together. I suspect if you had mentioned my project with the soldiers instead of my extravagant spending"—here she narrowed her eyes at him, and he had the grace to look slightly shamefaced—"Bancroft would have taken the opportunity to cry off that much sooner."

"I confess that was my next topic of conversation, but for your sake I am glad it did not come to that.

I can imagine the look on Ophelia's face at the mere mention of soldiers. If she is so condemning of animals, make no mistake, she would be convinced that soldiers returning from war would all carry fleas and be breeders of some dreadful foreign diseases." Max chuckled softly at the thought.

"It is no laughing matter," she said, although there was a suggestion of a grin in the set of her lips. Eventually she gained control and looked at him with a wistful expression in her eyes. "I am very sorry, sir, but it does not appear that I will be marrying as soon as you hoped."

"Such a shame, poppet," he said. Carefully he pulled her into the circle of his arms, wanting nothing more than to comfort her. But her nearness was much too tempting, and throwing caution to the wind, he bent his head and took possession of the inviting cherry lips.

A sigh of pure contentment escaped Amity as Max's lips touched hers. For a moment she accepted his embrace, welcoming the feeling of security that enveloped her body. She wished she could tell him how much she loved him, but she knew that was impossible. Despair filled her, and she became aware of the impropriety of her actions. Abruptly she broke the contact and pushed him away.

"Please, Max," she whispered. "You mustn't do that."

"Why ever not?" he asked, keeping his voice carefully neutral. "Don't you like it when I kiss you?"

"Yes, but it is not fitting," was the prim response.

"Surely between friends it would be suitable to share a kiss. As we did once before," he prodded, unsure whether he was going too fast. She had not seemed disgusted by his kiss, but she had not given him any encouragement either.

"That should not have happened, Max," Amity said, blushing in remembrance of his kiss in the river. She dropped her eyes and stared intently at the pattern of the carpet. "I did not wish to mention it at the time, but it was most improper of me to accept your embrace. After all, you will be offering for Honoria, and I cannot think that she would approve of your actions."

Amity's words were spoken so softly that Max had to bend his head to catch all of them. A wave of flowery scent wafted up to him, surrounding him in a magical spell as he inhaled the girl's fragrance. He had to clear the dryness from his throat before he was able to answer her.

"Perhaps you are right. However, I see little need to concern ourselves about her approval," he said, taking her hand once more.

"How so?" Amity asked, raising her head in confusion.

"I fear that I will not be offering for Miss Waterston," he said quietly. If he had not been holding her hand, Max might have missed the slight tremor that passed through her body. His own heartbeat increased to a terrifying rate, and his eyes took on a luminous sheen as he stared at her lovely face.

Amity could barely speak for the pounding of her heart at his words. She did not know what this rejection of Honoria portended, yet a thrill of excitement pulsed through her veins. She moistened her lips before she could speak. "I thought Honoria was the perfect lady."

"No, Amity, she was never perfect. For a while I thought she was." Green eyes locked with blue as he raised her hand to his lips. "You see, my dear, my peaceful life was invaded by a real lady, although at first I was hardly aware of that fact. I suspect this is perhaps a poor time to mention it, but I would be deeply honored if you would give some thought to the idea of marrying me."

Although his words created a burst of happiness in her chest, still she hesitated. She wanted so badly to think that his words and actions meant he had some feeling for her, but she could not trust her own reactions. She had been so long without love that she was frightened that she was imagining his affection. Amity's eyes searched his face, wanting to believe his words. She was so afraid to give him any encouragement for fear he might discover eventually she was everything he did not want in a wife. Reluctantly she pulled her hand from his, moving slightly away from him, aware of her own weakness at his nearness.

"Bancroft wanted to marry me, too," she said miserably. "But he soon discovered I was not the person he wanted. Once you think about it, you will see that we will never suit."

"Of course, we will suit. We are perfect for each other," Max said, wondering why she was being so stubborn. He reached out to grab her shoulders, wanting to convince her, but he stopped before he touched her. The feel of her body beneath his hands turned his mind to jelly. He folded his arms across his chest so that he would be more able to argue his case. "I have truly given this a great deal of thought, Amity. I honestly want to marry you because I think you would be the perfect wife."

"You have told me often enough that I do not behave as I should. You will be angry when I do not conform to society's rules," she accused him sadly.

"I probably will be angry. And at other times I will be bewildered. I will grump and grouse and love every minute of the confusion you spread around you. Don't you understand, my dear, that I really do want to marry you?"

"Why?"

Her question caught him off guard. What did she mean? Didn't she understand that he was in love with her? Then in a quick flash of humor at his own idiocy, he realized that he had only told her that he wanted to marry her. Exasperation at his own cautious nature infuriated him. Even if it was too soon to speak of love, he must be honest with her. He must risk everything if he wanted to win the prize. This time he did not hesitate as he reached out to grasp her shoulders and turn her toward him.

"The reason you must marry me is that my life will be impossible without you," he said. "You see, my dear, I have fallen in love with you."

Amity's mouth opened in a silent O of amazement, and it was all Max could do not to press a kiss to her soft lips. He felt his senses expanding, and he tried to control his thoughts, but they scattered before the assault on his emotions. Then he realized that it was the one sure way he could tell her of his feelings, and he touched her lips with his.

The kiss was the tenderest of salutes, but it offered a promise of delights beyond imagination.

If Max had questioned Amity's feelings, her reaction to this kiss convinced him that she reciprocated his feelings in full measure. This knowledge sent a devastating burst of passion through his body, and he groaned, pushing her away.

"We mustn't do that," he said primly.

"Why ever not? Don't you like to kiss me?" she asked cheekily.

"Behave yourself, you bold minx." He hastily stood up, glowering down at her wide-spread smile. "As your guardian I need to ask if you have considered the offer of marriage you have just received."

"Yes, Max, I have." Amity's eyes shone with an almost magical blue light.

"And will you accept the offer?"

"With all my heart," she said. She leaped to her feet and threw her arms around him, resting her cheek on the cool satin of his waistcoat. "On the condition, of course, that you have no objection to filthy and disease-ridden animals."

A rumble of laughter welled up in Max's throat as he thought of the pompous Bancroft Paige. The poor sod had no idea he had given up the perfect fiancée. "Yes, my dear, you may keep that mangy dog."

"And Ginger?"

"That is much to ask, but I will admit she did me a singular service." He sighed heavily as he pulled Amity closer. "Yes, you may keep Ginger."

"And Primrose?"

Max grasped her shoulders and pushed her away,

narrowing his eyes at the guileless blue eyes raised to his. "And who may I ask is Primrose?"

"A cow," Amity said, her lips trembling at the expression of disbelief on his face. "She's awfully sweet. And Dobson thinks she is quite healthy, even though her calf is due any day now."

"I will not have a cow drop a calf in my garden storeroom!" Max roared.

"Of course not, darling," Amity said as she placed her arms around his neck.

"And you will no longer pick up every stray animal in London!" he demanded.

"I promise, my dear," she said sliding her fingers into the shining thatch of chestnut hair. "Unless, of course. . . ."

A low groan issued from his throat. "I know. Unless they really need a good home."

Even as he lowered his head, Max suspected that the years ahead might be long indeed. But there would be joy unsuspected in every day.